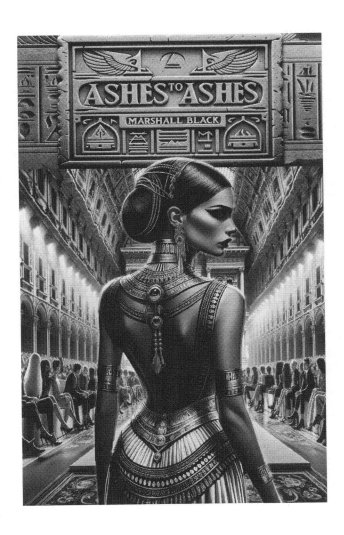

Ashes to Ashes
Book 3A A Mike McHaskell Novella
Marshall Black

McHaskell Enterprises

Prologue -The Ptolemaic Dynasty:

A chariot raced through the dusty streets at dawn, drawn by four magnificent white stallions. Each breath they took seemed ablaze with fire in the early morning light. Keryx, the official messenger and announcer of the Macedonian army, dismounted with a grave expression. It was the year 323 BC, and he had come to deliver news of a profound tragedy that had struck the Kingdom.

Gathering the townspeople in the center, his voice rang out, "Hear ye, hear ye! A somber shadow has been cast upon us. Alexander the Great, the King of Kings and conqueror of nations, has taken his final breath. Let your tears flow like rivers, but do not let them extinguish the flames of his enduring legacy. He, who bent empires to his will and challenged fate itself, now rests among the gods. Keep him alive in your hearts, for his spirit will eternally gallop through the heavens!"

General Leonidas, his face etched with solemnity, approached Ptolemy, the King's second in command. The dust of the camp clung to his armor, a testament to the haste of his journey. He stood before Ptolemy, a man still unaware of the seismic shift about to upend the world he knew.

"Strategos Ptolemy," Leonidas began, his voice steady despite the weight of his message. "I bring grave tidings from Babylon. Alexander, our King and leader, has breathed his last. The world we fought to conquer now teeters on the brink of an uncertain future."

Ptolemy, taken aback, remained silent for a moment, absorbing the magnitude of these words. The death of Alexander was not just the end of a man but the end of an era. And in that silence, the seeds of a new destiny began to sprout.

Leonidas continued, with a mixture of reverence and urgency in his tone, "My King, in this moment of turmoil and transition, what would be your command?"

Ptolemy found himself suddenly thrust into an unprecedented position. His friend and brother-in-arms, Alexander, was no more, leaving the immense weight of the vast empire resting squarely on his shoulders. While he grieved silently for his fallen friend, he knew he had to press on. With resolve in his voice, Ptolemy declared, "Leonidas, now we must begin the transformation of Egypt. From this day forth, the Ptolemaic Dynasty shall rise. Long live the memory of our fallen King. With the help of the gods, we will honor his legacy, my brother."

Approximately 254 years after Alexander's death, a baby girl was delivered into a world vastly different from the one he had known. She was destined to become the last Pharaoh of Egypt. Born into the Ptolemaic Dynasty and descended from the line of the great King of Kings, this child was Cleopatra. She would one day rise as the mighty Queen of the Nile. Her ascent to the throne marked both the pinnacle and the twilight of an era.

In 31 BC, the Battle of Actium marked a defining moment in history. It proved to be the final chapter in the famed reign of the Egyptian Pharaohs. From that point forward, the once-great nation of Egypt would exist under the rule of foreign powers, its era of independence and majestic rule drawing to a close.

The renowned conqueror Octavian, later known as Augustus the Mighty, new Caesar of the Roman Empire, decreed that all offspring of the once powerful Queen Cleopatra be brought to Rome. This was to be a display of dominance over the fallen Kingdom of Egypt. Upon hearing this news, the now defeated Cleopatra, alongside her lover Mark Antony, in a final act of defiance and despair, took their own lives in the year 30 BC.

Tasked with solemn duty, the formidable Legionary Legate Gaius Claudius Sicilius entered the city of Alexandria to execute his orders. His Mission was to escort the young offspring of Cleopatra, the last remnants of a bygone era, to Rome. However, neither Gaius nor her descendants ever arrived in the Imperial City. Legend has it that they were lost at sea, victims of a divine storm. Their ship, caught in the treacherous Strait of Messina, was said to have been swallowed by The Great Twins, Scylla, and Charybdis—the six-headed sea monster and a voracious whirlpool. This feared passage had claimed many men, ships, and treasures in its tumultuous waters.

Contrary to the widespread legend, the ship was not lost, as so many had believed. There are tales that speak of a different fate, one where a sense of moral duty or perhaps a deep compassion for the innocent prevailed. The Legionary Legate Gaius Claudius Sicilius and his precious cargo did not perish in the sea as foretold. Instead, he is said to have made a daring escape to his ancestral lands in Sicily. According to legend, Gaius and his wife, Livia, secretly raised the children in the shelter of Sicily's rolling hills, away from the prying eyes of Rome. The legacy of the great Pharaohs of Egypt was said to have lived on and nurtured under the care of their new protectors.

Saint Christopher:

Sangin, Helmand Province Afghanistan, May 2003:

The sound of small arms fire filled the air, the telltale whizzing of bullets, and the unmistakable thud they made hitting the ground and walls shocked Markus into terror. As a Specialized Skills Officer (SSO), Agent Delphy was trained for high-risk, covert operations, possessing skills in intelligence gathering, advanced combat, and strategic planning. Despite his extensive training, this was his first time in actual battle, and the reality was far more challenging than any simulation.

"Goddamn it, Markus! Get your shit together. Take what you can carry and leave the rest!" Master Chief Maximilian Colburn Sr. yelled out. He was determined to pull his men out of this 'fucked-up' situation.

The team was part of Operation Thunderbolt, a joint military operation conducted by the United States and Afghan forces in Afghanistan, launched in May 2003. The troops cleared numerous caves, tunnels, and homes, destroying caches of weapons and ammunition. Markus's job was to collect any intel and decipher what he could, then report to the higher-ups on their findings. Today, they had stumbled upon a treasure trove of intelligence – locations, caches, and plots. One particularly interesting bit involved the Chinese government. Markus had proof that the Ministry of State Security (MSS), China's equivalent of the CIA, had provided crucial intelligence to the Taliban by giving them access to their surveillance system. The Chinese Yaogan (□□) reconnaissance satellite constellation, while not as accurate as the U.S. National Reconnaissance Office's fleet, was still quite effective. This intelligence needed to be protected at all costs, and Markus wasn't about to let this slip through his fingers.

Master Chief Colburn Sr. had been with the Navy for over a decade. His tenure on SEAL Team 3 Echo Platoon had mainly involved training. In 1990, when Saddam Hussein invaded Kuwait, SEAL Team Echo was stationed just outside of Kuwait City. Despite their eagerness to join the fight, they were on stand-down, leading to pent-up anger with no outlet. Eleven years later, Max Sr., alongside his sons Max Jr. and Mike, his adopted son, watched in horror as the Twin Towers fell on September 11, 2001. From that day forward, Master Chief Colburn Sr. found himself an outlet for his skills and determination, and it was indeed a significant one.

"Yes, Chief. I just need to get everything out," Markus exclaimed, quickly grabbing all the paperwork he could handle. Men were shouting; bullets were flying—the sounds of war unforgettable to anyone who's heard them. Every explosion, gunshot, and battle cry left its mark.

The Team was pinned down, having moved from the small village of Sangin in Helmand Province. The Taliban, aware of the SEALs' skills, had devised a simple yet effective plan of attack: flood the field with bodies. Taliban commanders, understanding that most of their warriors would fall to the Americans, hoped some would hit their mark. Now, aided by new Chinese intelligence, this was precisely what was happening at that very moment.

However, their plan needed to be executed swiftly. The U.S. Air Force would be on target in mere moments, bringing extinction from above. The

"Angel of Death" was en route. Lockheed's AC-130 Gunship was a heavily armed, four-engine turboprop aircraft designed for close air support, air interdiction, and armed reconnaissance. The AC-130 had a formidable arsenal, including 105mm and 40mm cannons, Gatling guns, and missiles.

Senior Chief Petty Officer Christopher Canepa had located an exfiltration point. The men would have to scale a thousand-foot cliff to the south, where Blackhawk helicopters would await their arrival. He relayed this vital information to the Master Chief.

Suddenly, a Taliban rocket-propelled grenade (RPG) found its mark. The men were barricaded in what was now an "abandoned home," which boasted a large courtyard surrounded by thick stone walls. This was unusual for the area; most were made from mud-brick, not stone. These walls offered the perfect shield to the small arms fire wielded against the SEALs.

Senior Chief Juan Santiago was instantly killed as shrapnel tore through the side of his vest. His body fell onto Markus, who was gathering the last bits of intel from the office they were in. The house had once belonged to Mullah Abdul Rahman, "The Darkness" Khan, believed to be the Taliban's link with the Chinese. Khan was a man of considerable means; his family was deeply involved in the expansive poppy-growing business. Opium, an extremely lucrative commodity in Afghanistan, had been and continued to be the cornerstone of their wealth.

What happened next would forever haunt Markus Delphy. Senior Chief Petty Officer Canepa sprinted toward his fallen teammate. Seconds later, darkness engulfed the room. Smoke and dust filled the air, mingling with the metallic scent of war. To this day, Markus remembers only fragments: no sound, no screams, just fleeting glimpses of blackness.

"So, what do you think, Worm?" Markus was disoriented, struggling to comprehend the sudden shift. Moments before, he had been in the throes of battle, his life in the hands of the men sworn to protect him. Now, abruptly, he found himself back at the Forward Operating Base (FOB). 'What the hell?' he murmured, his voice laced with confusion.

Canepa examined him, a mixture of concern and excitement in his eyes. "Worm, I mean my new daughter. What do you think? Her eyes are amazing, yes?"

Still grappling with the abrupt change in his surroundings, Markus asked, "Chris, what happened? Weren't we just in a firefight?"

"Haha, Worm in a firefight? Yeah, that'll be the day," laughed Senior Chief Santiago. Markus turned to see his friend very much alive, lounging on his rack and casually flipping through one of his "magazines."

Petey chuckled, echoing Santiago. He was captivated by his latest acquisition. The team had gifted him a sort of memento from their training Mission in the Orient—a chrome-plated lighter. Despite the engraving being a "dig" at him, he cherished it all the same. A gift from his brothers was always welcome.

"Jesus, Juan, Pete, you're okay?" Relief washed over Markus as he turned back to the Senior Chief. "Seriously, Chris, what is going on?"

Canepa answered with a puzzled look, "I don't know what you are talking about, brother. We just got here yesterday. We haven't even crossed the wire yet. Are you okay? Maybe you downed too many of Petey's cocktails last night."

Every member of the team had a nickname. Take Petey, for instance. While on a training Mission in Singapore, Special Warfare Operator 3rd Class Peter Jenson visited a place where sailors often sought companionship on lonely nights. His teammates decided to surprise Jenson, and when they did, the woman he was with struggled with some English words. Instead of 'penis,' she referred to it as his 'small Petey.' The name stuck.

As for Worm, Markus earned that nickname due to his tendency to always have his head buried in a book. Completely absorbed in his reading, he delved into everything from warfare strategy to manuals on code deciphering. The nickname 'Worm' was born, and it was a title Agent Markus Delphy wore with pride.

Senior Chief Canepa's nickname had its own unique origin. Born in Novara di Sicilia, a quaint town near Messina in Sicily, Canepa grew up on an olive orchard where his family had produced olive oil for centuries. At fourteen, he moved to the United States, settling with family in Brooklyn, New York. There, Christopher Canepa fell in love with America and swiftly integrated into its culture. Years later, he found himself in the Navy, serving his adopted country in Afghanistan.

His teammates, aware of his immigrant status, jokingly dubbed him 'WOP'—an old, often derogatory term implying 'without papers.' However, Canepa embraced this nickname as a badge of honor, a symbol of his journey and the new life he had built.

Chris was a man of smaller stature, standing at a mere 5'5", but he was built like a tugboat. His striking blue eyes and unforgettable smile had captured the heart of Valentina Fiore, his first and only true love. Christopher and Valentina married right out of high school. The couple welcomed their first child, a baby girl, just two days after the Senior Chief deployed. "So, what do you think, Worm?" he repeated, gesturing towards the photo of his beautiful new little girl, who shared their combined name. Christina.

Markus, still unsure if this was real or a dream, replied, "She's beautiful, Chris, really beautiful. And those eyes, my God, she has your eyes."

"I know. There's no mistaking who her father is, that's for sure," Canepa's face shifted from elation to longing. "I just wish I could have met her."

"What do you mean, you redeploy home in a few weeks? That's not that long; hang in there, buddy."

The room suddenly plunged back into darkness. Markus, startled, glanced around, trying to adjust his eyes to the stark change. To his astonishment, Senior Chief Santiago and Petey were nowhere to be seen. The two men were now standing alone in an eerily empty tent. The Senior Chief's voice continued, a chill ran down Markus's spine. "Markus, we're not really here. We're still in that hell; at least you are. I have a favor to ask. Please, watch over my wife and my baby; she's going to need a father now. Keep them safe, promise me, brother."

Canepa then pulled something out of his pocket and gently placed it in Markus's hand, closing his fingers over it with a sense of purpose. "Give this to my little girl; tell her it's from me, that it will protect her. Tell them both I'm in a good place now—no pain, no sorrow, that I love them and will always be watching over them. Can you do this for me, Markus?" His words were a heartfelt plea, echoing in the quiet of the darkness.

"Chris, I don't understand. What's going on?"

"Brother, all will be made clear shortly," Chris smiled before continuing, "You are going to have an interesting life, my friend, a very interesting one."

As Markus heard those words, the distant yet unmistakable sounds of war started to echo around him, intensifying at that very moment.

"Markus! Markus! Wake up, you're okay. Come on, wake up!" someone was urgently shouting at him. Sand and dust whipped across his face; he could feel the gritty particles, but his eyes were shrouded in darkness. Both his hands were trapped, but he couldn't discern what was pinning them down. With a determined effort, he managed to free his left hand and remove the obstruction from his eyes.

He was on the floor of the exfil helicopter, sand blowing in from outside as the aircraft climbed into the sky. He turned his head and spotted a medic tending to Chief Colburn Sr., wrapping his arm in bandages. Slowly moving his head around, he saw three other team members: Johnson, Reynolds, and Martinez. His right hand remained immobile, and moments later, he understood why. Three lifeless bodies were crammed onto the floor space: Senior Chief Juan Santiago, Special Warfare Operator 3rd Class Peter Jenson, and his friend, Senior Chief Petty Officer Christopher Canepa, had all given their lives for their country that day. They had made the ultimate sacrifice to save him.

When he finally freed his right hand, he discovered he was tightly clutching something. With deliberate care, Markus slowly opened each finger, revealing a precious treasure in his palm—a necklace adorned with a gleaming gold medallion. It depicted a heroic man, his muscular frame and long, flowing beard, carrying a child upon his shoulder while holding a sturdy staff in his hand. It was Saint Christopher, the revered Patron Saint of Travelers.

I'm Starving!:

Present Day:

"Alright, alright, you win, uncle. I give up," Mike declared, his tone a blend of surrender and levity.

Mike and Christina were traveling by train through Europe. They were aboard the famous Venice Simplon-Royal-Express. The couple was celebrating their third wedding anniversary and their second honeymoon. The route followed the renowned journey from Paris to Milan.

They had been given the most elaborate of gifts. Markus Delphy, the Director of the Central Intelligence Agency and one of Mike's best friends, purchased the couple their fare. Not just any accommodations either, he went all out, reserving the Royal Windsor Suite.

The Royal Windsor Suite, an entire rail car, a fusion of wood and steel reminiscent of a bygone era, was meticulously crafted for the utmost luxury. Inside, the living area boasted a snooker table, four plush chairs, and a minibar filled with the finest elixirs. Extravagant wood carvings embellished the walls, harmonizing with opulent curtains framing the large windows just below the skylights that enveloped most of the curved ceiling. The combination displayed breathtaking scenes of nature, offering a one-of-a-kind moving panorama of Europe's most stunning landscapes and unequaled experiences of the night skies.

The car was cleverly divided, with the rear half transformed into a master suite. It was the epitome of extravagance, featuring a king-sized bed with the finest linens, a spacious bathroom, and a dressing area with 360-degree lighted viewing mirrors. The Royal Windsor Suite was strategically positioned at the train's end and included an enclosed platform. This allowed the couple to take in the most stunning and uninterrupted views of Europe and the majestic French and Italian Alps. It was as if they were royalty in a fairytale.

Christina's laughter was light and teasing as she replied, "I tried to warn you, husband. I'm in the best shape of my life. No way you could keep up with me, old man. Plus, you had fun, even if you did 'surrender.'" She gave him a playful wink.

Mike retorted with a grin, "Surrender? Never, my Queen. Surrender isn't in my vocabulary! Now, where were we?"

Their laughter filled the room, a reminder of the joy they found in each other's company. This trip was their first alone since their fateful honeymoon in Tokyo, and Mike pulled out all the stops.

Christina halted his advance with a playful hand, "Ah, before you have a heart attack, how about some food? I'm starving. We've been cooped up in here since we left Paris. I need to eat if I'm going to keep up my 'energy,'" she said with a teasing glance.

Mike was more than relieved by the suggestion. He was utterly exhausted and welcomed the break. "Of course, Babe. Let me get us some dinner. What would my Queen like?" he asked, wanting to cater to her every wish.

"A burger, big, juicy, and delicious. Oh, and bacon, lots of bacon. Fries, and maybe even a malt, chocolate or strawberry. Don't bother if it's vanilla.

That's a waste." Christina's eyes glistened with anticipation of her impending meal.

"Then I'll go. Now you just lay down and rest, my wife. You're gonna need it." Mike turned to get dressed.

"Hmm, well, okay then. I will. But, Mike, I'll need to get up sometime, you know, like, to go potty."

"How about you just give it a few more minutes? I'll be right back," Mike said as he exited the bedroom.

Life for Mike McHaskell had come together nicely; there was a noticeable spring in his step. His mind was, for once, clear, and happy thoughts were commonplace. *And why not? I am happily married to five beautiful women, all of whom I have excellent relationships with. Why not be happy?* Of course, if he was being honest with himself, not all five were so perfect. In fact, his marriage to Elena was in trouble.

The couple, in reality, Elena, had made a choice: She would live in Europe and continue her job, while Mike would remain in Texas with the other wives and the family's growing number of children. Mike would travel to Paris every three months, spend a week there, and then return home. Elena would travel to the States and spend time with the family as her position allowed. On paper, it worked; in reality, it did not.

Life got in the way for the couple. Mike's home commitments, mainly because his wives were in various states of pregnancy, kept his days busy. Claire and Bailey had decided how many children they each wanted, which gave both Christina and Parker chills. Claire was already a mother to Rebecca and Timothy Michael and had just given birth to Robert James a few months ago. Christina gave him William and then Mike's namesake,

Michael Jr., who just had his first birthday the day before the couple headed out on this trip. Parker gave him another son, Edward. Bailey's first child was also a boy, Thomas Jefferson, and she is pregnant with the couple's next child, yet another boy, Peter Michael. Mike and Elena, again mostly Elena, had chosen not to have any children, and as of late, that has been the course.

Yes, for Mike McHaskell, life was great. He was on a train trip across Europe with the love of his life, and his home life was equally amazing. He was impossibly happy.

However, as the saying goes, "A bright sunny day can turn in an instant. So always carry your umbrella." Sadly for Mike, he had forgotten his.

As he walked into the dining car, he was met by the hostess. Her name badge read Monique; under her name was where she called home, Montpellier, France.

"Hello Seer, 'ow can I 'elp you tonight?" asked Monique.

"Hello, I need to order something to go. Where do I do that?" Mike answered.

"Oui, please follow moi, you order at zee counter. Zis way."

Mike nodded in appreciation to the woman as she returned to her station after guiding him. True to his "nature," he couldn't resist a quick glance as she walked away.

"Damn, Mike, five wives still isn't enough for you? Jeez, man, that's rough," commented a man sitting at the counter.

Mike instantly recognized the voice; it was one he didn't want to hear, especially while on vacation. "Damn it, Casey, why the hell are you here?" he asked.

Agent Casey Green, also known as the 'Shadow,' sat at the counter, his face concealed behind a newspaper. Slowly, he lowered it onto the counter. "Hey Mike, I didn't know you and Christina were on vacation. Sorry for interrupting, brother. But listen, Markus sent me, and I honestly didn't know."

Agent Green could be summed up in one word: 'classic.' He was the embodiment of a 'Secret Agent' or 'Gray-man.' He looked and dressed the part, from his slicked-back hair to his dark gray trench coat. Next to his cup of coffee, there was even a matching fedora sitting on the counter. The quintessential TV detective described Agent Casey Green of the Central Intelligence Agency.

"You didn't know? How is that possible? This train is full of newlyweds or people, well, like Christina and me, you know, trying to get 'alone time.' How long have you been on this train?"

"That's the shitty part. Markus didn't tell me about any of that. I just hopped aboard on the first stop after you left Paris yesterday. When I figured out what this," he motioned around the dining car, "place was about, I thought I would give you two some time together before... you know, I messed things up."

Mike shook his head, "Ahhh, Markus. I should have known. It's okay, Casey, what's the message?"

"Actually, it's this," Agent Green reached into his coat pocket and removed a sat phone. "He wants you to call him."

After taking the phone from his uninvited guest, Mike found a quiet place to call the Director. He did his best to keep his temper in check, although he was quickly losing the battle. "Markus, you sent Casey to find me? This better be good, brother, really good," anger evident in his tone and volume.

Director Markus Delphy replied, "Alright, settle down and keep that Irish temper at bay. Yes, I did, and I promise this is an easy one. I need you to pick up a case for us. No big deal, a milk run."

"Pick up a case? What case? And where do I find this case?"

"That's the best part, Mike, it's on the train. Our old friend Alessandro is traveling with it to Milan just like you are. You see, milk run, just like I said."

Alessandro Romano Vitali, or simply Alessandro, as he was known to those in his orbit, was what certain individuals referred to as a 'Procure-ment Specialist.' When contracted, Alessandro had the unique skill of locating whatever one needed and acquiring items that, let's just say, would be difficult to obtain through normal channels.

Mike and Alessandro had a storied relationship; neither man trusted the other much. But they did have a working understanding. The CIA re-quired Alessandro's help from time to time, and this brought Mike and him together on occasion.

"Of course, I should have known." Mike shook his head as he spoke. "You know, Markus, I never had the chance to thank you for the tickets you bought Christina and me for our anniversary. Thank you. Brother... Dude, you're getting more and more like Albert every day."

"Mike, that was uncalled for. Okay, yes, I had an ulterior motive for giving you those tickets. But I promise it will be an easy job. Just get me that case, and then you can go back to your vacation. Besides, Alessandro is a lover, not a fighter. Isn't that what he always says?"

"Fine, Markus. You win. So what's in the case?"

"Don't worry about what's in it. Just get it for me. Alessandro already has a buyer, so you will need to up the bid. I'll okay up to $15M, but not a penny more. Intel says the bid is currently at 10, so that should be enough. Get it done, Mike."

"Markus, you know I will. What about the other buyer? Aren't they gonna be pissed with us just screwing them out of this case?"

"Alessandro works for us, Mike. We have priority status; that was the agreement made with him. If his current customer is upset, so be it. Call me when it's done, and thank you, Brother. Sorry for the deception."

"That's okay, Markus, but I will remember this and for a very long time." Mike hung up the phone and returned to the dining car.

"Monique, hello again. Hey, I hope you can help me. My friend Alessandro Vitali. Does he have a reservation for tonight? You see, my wife and I were supposed to eat with him, and she wasn't feeling very well, so I canceled. But she just told me she feels much better, and I hope to change the reservation back to the three of us tonight. I just don't know what time he will be here. Can you help me out?"

As he spoke, he slid a hundred-dollar bill across her podium. Monique smiled and gave him a wink.

"But of course," she ran her fingers down the reservation book, "Ah, 'ere it ees. Oui, 'e will be in zee main dining car in forty-five minutes. But monsieur, it is black tie. I am afraid your current attire will not suffize."

"That will be fine, thank you, Monique. You've been a big help." Mike gave her his shit-eating grin, a smile that could melt the heart of any woman—all except Claire, especially when she knew he was up to no good.

Of Course I Knew:

Mike eased the bedroom door open, careful not to make a sound as he stepped into the railcar. His hands were empty, a fact Christina was not going to appreciate. Although not entirely without, he had snagged a package of oyster crackers Agent Green had left next to a cleared bowl of bisque.

Upon entering, he realized the bed was not occupied. Christina was in the bathroom.

Hearing him come in, she called out, "Hey, you're back! Great, I'm starving." Her voice filtered through the bathroom door, a mix of relief and hunger.

Mike replied, "Babe, slight change of plans."

There was a brief pause before what he expected occurred. Christina threw back the bathroom door, standing there in her birthday suit, which always left him speechless. However, this time, she wasn't so happy to see him.

"What do you mean 'change of plans?' I told you that I was hungry, and you promised to get me something to eat. Come on, Mike, it's been like 24 hours now. And this crap," she motioned to the empty plates of 'finger foods' around the room, "sucked. They were like eating air. What's wrong with these people? Don't they know what real food is?"

Christina made it painfully obvious that she was hungry, upset with him, and ready to explode.

Trying to appease the brewing storm that was Christina, Mike handed her the unopened package of crackers. "I got these for you," he said with a hopeful but sheepish look.

She snatched the package from his hand, then returned to her death stare. "So what's the change of plans?" she asked, speaking through a mouth full of crackers.

"Well, I thought, since it's our last night on the train, how about we go for a nice dinner? I made reservations for the Main Dining car. You'll love it, Babe—all the food you want to eat, drinks, music. Come on, let's do it. After all, it's our second honeymoon. I want to see my wife all dressed up."

"Dressed up? What do you mean, dressed up? Mike, we've been pretty busy for the last day. I need a shower, and *you*, need a shower," she stepped forward to give him a sniff and then stepped back, "Yeah, definitely a shower. You smell like sex and maple syrup," she paused for a second, "Really, I just wanted to relax tonight, maybe watch something on my iPad, you know, relax. Not get all dressed up."

By the look on Mike's face, Christina could tell he really wanted to do this. And, like always, she gave in. "Okay, fine, I'll go. Give me an hour, and I'll be ready. Good thing you at least, and I mean the very least, got me those crackers." She walked back into the bathroom and closed the door.

Mike now had to break the news: not an hour, but less than 40 minutes.

He spoke to her through the door, "Babe, one more thing..."

"You've got to be fucking kidding me! Do you have any clue how long it takes for me to bathe, dry my hair, get dressed, and put on makeup... Mike, you're absolutely out of your mind!" Christina unleashed a three-minute tirade while frenziedly sifting through the suite, yanking clothes from the armoire, and then flinging open the closet to reveal Mike's tuxedo. With a dramatic gesture towards it, she was suddenly back in the bathroom, door slamming shut behind her, as a stream of colorful expletives continued to flow seamlessly, all aimed squarely at Mike. He couldn't help but burst into laughter. Mike was absolutely smitten with his wife; she was his entire universe, and her fiery temper was one of the things he adored most about her.

"Honey, I'll make it up to you; thank you for doing this," was all he could say.

After he dressed, things had calmed down. The shower was now off, and he could hear the hairdryer blowing. Mike found a quiet spot to wait, thinking it was better not to say anything and just let her be. Moments later, Christina opened the bathroom door just enough to stick her arm out. In her hand was deodorant and a small bottle of Mike's cologne.

"Here, you stink. Use it," she said as she shook the items at him.

"Thank you, Babe," Mike retrieved.

This time, she left the door partially ajar, almost enough for him to get a glimpse inside, but not quite.

"By the way, I know what you're doing, Mike."

"What I'm doing?" he asked, confused.

"Yes, I know what you're doing. It's been a year since Mikey was born, so you think it's time."

This caught Mike off guard. He thought he had been sly, maneuvering in a way that would leave her none the wiser. In reality, Christina had picked up on his intent right away. Mike wasn't as stealthy as he believed himself to be. In fact, among the wives, it was a running joke about how transparent he truly was, never quite managing to pull the wool over their eyes. Of course, the exception was the secret of his true identity. Though truth be told, that wasn't as well-guarded of a mystery as he liked to think it was either.

Claire had a few quirks, one of which she took very seriously was the family's health. She grew the food she could and insisted on buying organic for everything else. She also had an extreme position on birth control in the house, specifically that no synthetic hormones would be allowed. This meant only mechanical forms of contraception were permissible. She feared these hormones could pass through the mother's milk and into the children.

This posed a problem for Christina, as she was allergic to latex. Not that it would have mattered anyway; she despised the feeling of condoms and thus wouldn't let Mike use them. But she also didn't want to get pregnant right away again, something that Mike always seemed to manage to do to her.

So, the couple resorted to the 'controlled approach,' or 'coitus interruptus,' in medical terms. This had worked for the past year, although the couple had a few "near misses," as Christina would say, due to Mike's inability to "control himself." However, for the past week, all precautions were gone. Mike was back to his old ways, and it came as no surprise to Christina.

"Umm, I don't know what to say, Babe..."

Christina swung the door wide open. She was a vision, adorned in a stunning pristine white v-neck split-thigh backless elegant gown that draped over her figure flawlessly. Mike stood there, utterly awestruck by the beauty before him. Her hair was swept to one side in a style reminiscent of 1930s sex symbols, adding an air of classic elegance to her modern beauty.

Her lips, painted in dark red matte lipstick, formed a smile that made his heart skip a beat. The shade highlighted the contours of her lips that he so loved to kiss.

But above all, what truly captivated him were Christina's most prized possessions – her magnificent dark blue eyes that seemed to hold the universe within.

As Mike stood there stunned, she continued, "Of course, I knew. I'm not an idiot. It's okay, Mike. I'm ready, too. You know, all you had to do was ask; I've been ready for a while now."

"Umm... You were? You are?" Mike asked, still trying to process her words.

Christina walked over to him. "Here, let me fix your tie," she said as she straightened his collar. "Oh, my husband, why do you play such games? Look, we've already discussed having more children, and I agreed. Not as many as Claire or Bailey; they are out of their freakin minds, but a few more is okay."

"Honey, I'm sorry. I should've talked to you about it. I just thought if it was a surprise... then..."

"Surprise? Come on, Mike, what were you planning? To have another 'accident'? Maybe a few more times?" She chuckled, brushing off his shoulders and straightening his jacket. "Really, it's okay. I'm ready." She gave him a wink. "Now, close your mouth before you drool all over your new tux," she teased, strutting out the door.

Someone Big in The Chinese Government:

Alessandro Romano Vitali was seated in the main dining car. A wealthy man, though not as affluent as the McHaskells, however, he was undoubtedly well-off. He enjoyed flaunting his fortune, surrounding himself with fast cars, glamorous women, and opulent homes on every continent except North America. And, of course, his attire was always first-rate and ideally suited to demonstrate his extravagant lifestyle.

He was clad in a custom-fit Brioni tuxedo, the epitome of Italian elegance and craftsmanship. The luxurious blend of wool and silk fabric caressed his body, accentuating his athletic physique. His tuxedo was a deep, rich black, creating a bold contrast with the pristine white of his shirt. The peak lapel, a classic detail, added a touch of sophistication, while the single-button fastening provided a modern twist. His shoes, handmade black leather Oxfords, shined to perfection and gleamed under the soft lights of the room. The matching black silk bow tie, white pocket square, and black diamond cufflinks were the perfect finishing touches to this ensemble, elevating his look to the pinnacle of sartorial excellence.

Alessandro fancied himself a kind of "Supervillain," although he was far from it. He wanted people to recognize him immediately; to achieve this, his lapel proudly displayed his signature emblem: one large, pristine, fresh white gardenia. The flower had been specially flown in from the gardens of the Amalfi Coast, its aromatic scent adding an extra layer of indulgence to his ensemble. As a symbol of purity and refinement, Alessandro believed the gardenia was the perfect reflection of his impeccable taste and wealth.

Mike and Christina entered the dining car, and he spotted Alessandro seated at a four-top table, just as requested, and led her to his mark. "Alessandro, well, fancy seeing you here! What a small world," he expressed as the couple approached.

Alessandro was caught off guard. Mike McHaskell wasn't someone you wanted to 'accidentally' run into. In fact, his orbit was somewhere you most definitely did not want to find yourself.

He replied, "Buonasera, Mike; it is a pleasure to see you again." His gaze then caught sight of what he considered the most beautiful woman he had ever seen. He couldn't help but ask, "And who is this goddess before me?" Alessandro slowly reached for her hand, holding it gently in both of his, while Christina started to answer. "Hello, I am...."

Mike cut in, "Alessandro, this is my wife, Christina."

This put Alessandro at ease. If Elena had been with Mike, his life would have been all but forfeit. But with Christina, he thought he might make it out of this meeting alive. "Christina, what a charming name. I am Alessandro Romano Vitali. I stand at your service. And may I say, Hai gli occhi più belli che abbia mai visto. (You have the most beautiful eyes I have ever seen)."

"Christina smiled, then returned the politeness, "Grazie, penso che i miei occhi siano la mia caratteristica più preziosa. (Thank you, I think my eyes are my most valuable feature)."

Of course, this took Mike by surprise; he had no idea that Christina spoke Italian, something he needed to find out more about. But before he could talk, Alessandro broke the short silence.

"I hardly believe that, Christina. I think you are hiding more assets than you let on," he said with a sly tone, his eyes scanning her from head to toe. Then, with a cunning smile, he added, "However, my dear, I suspect you already know this. And you speak Italian? Where did you learn my beautiful language? Your words were simply perfect."

Christina flashed her brighter-than-life smile, motioned to the chair, and asked, "May we sit?"

Alessandro, stunned that his manners were not up to his usual impeccable standards, replied, "Sì, sì, of course. Where are my manners? Please join me for dinner; you must." He quickly stepped around from the opposite side of the table, brushing Mike's hands away from Christina's chair, then pulled it out for her. Mike let out a slight chuckle, seeing him so disheveled - something that Alessandro never was. Of course, he had also never met Christina. She had that effect on every man she encountered.

After she was settled, Alessandro returned to his seat. Mike, still smiling, also sat. Alessandro asked, "Now, as you were saying? My language?"

"Yes, well, my birth father and mother were Italian. He was actually from Italy, but he died when I was very little. My mother believed it was important for me to understand my heritage, so she taught me the language of my ancestors. My father taught her, so it was kind of like he was talking to me. She also taught my sister Italian."

Mike was surprised by this new information. He was aware Claire understood some other languages, like French, but he had no idea she spoke

Italian and that Christina did too. This revelation prompted him to ask, "Honey, I didn't know you spoke Italian, and Claire does too. How am I just finding out about this?"

Christina turned to him and answered, "I don't know, maybe you just never asked. You know that Claire and I, as kids, traveled with our parents all over Europe. She also speaks French and German." She then addressed Alessandro, "My sister was quite the nerd. Actually, she still is. She was always trying to impress me with her brain. Come to think of it, she still does."

"German?" Mike was lost in thought. *What else don't I know about these two?* Honestly, It was his fault. Everyone he had ever met before—girlfriends, even Parker and Bailey—he had done a thorough and exhaustive background check on. But not his Claire or Christina. He thought he knew everything about them. *Guess I was wrong,* he mused.

"You know, my husband speaks that Gobbledygook. He flaunts it whenever we're with others who speak it too," Christina said with a laugh, then motioned for the waiter. "I'm hungry, Mike. Can we please order?" she asked.

"Of course, Babe," Mike answered as he raised his arm. He called out to get the waiter's attention, "Excuse me, sir!"

"I'm sorry. I am not familiar with such a term. Gobbledy...?" Alessandro's face showed his confusion.

Christina answered, "Gobbledygook. It's what Mike speaks when he talks to those Arab men. You know, their language. Mike is fluent in it."

"Ahhh, you mean Arabic. Yes, your husband is proficient in many..." Mike cut Alessandro off mid-sentence with a swift kick to his leg, followed by a stern glare. Alessandro returned to his speech, "It is wonderful to hear the words of my homeland coming from your mouth."

Christina didn't acknowledge his remarks or even notice the under-the-table exchange. She was hungry and frantically looking for the waiter to take her order. Finally, he arrived. Christina couldn't contain herself and blurted out, "I want a burger, huge! Juicy, with bacon, cheese, and whatever else you can find to put on it. Fries too. And please hurry. I'm dying here."

The shock and, quite frankly, the disdain on the man's face was palpable. "A hamburger? My dear, you are in the world's most illustrious five-star dining rail car. Should you desire such a... 'hamburger,'" he paused, seemingly battling the urge to retch, "then I must direct you out of this fine place. I assure you, that culinary monstrosity shall not sully the tables of this establishment, ever."

The man couldn't help but give her a once-over, his smugness practically oozing from his pores. Christina's expression morphed from hunger to something that screamed, *Those are fighting words.* Mike recognized that telltale glint in his wife's eyes, knowing she was teetering on the brink of an explosive tirade. She coiled up like a snake poised to strike and blurted out, "You French piece of shi..."

Alessandro swiftly intervened, effortlessly switching to French, the waiter's native tongue, solidifying his claim as the world's best Procurement Specialist. "Monsieur, the lady here has requested her dinner, which is precisely what she shall receive," he stated with authority, his gaze firmly locked on target. The waiter could feel the intensity of the glares from both men, accompanied by the young lady's scathing look. "I trust you grasp the gravity of your situation. Now, be so kind as to relay to the chef that he is to prepare for her the most delectable hamburger he has ever had the pleasure of crafting. Simply put, tell him his culinary prowess—and, indeed, your very 'livelihood'—are hanging in the balance. Capisce?"

The waiter nodded, not saying a word, and scurried off toward the kitchen. Alessandro turned to Christina, "There. It is all taken care of, my dear. A hamburger you shall receive."

"Thank you, Alessandro, that was very kind of you." Christina turned to Mike, "Honey, I need to use the ladies' room. I'll be right back."

Before Mike could stand to pull out her chair, Alessandro jumped up from his, bumping the table with his knees, although it didn't faze him. He moved over quickly to Christina, offered his hand, and held her chair out for her. "Signora, your destination is in the far corner," he motioned to the end of the railcar. Christina smiled at him and then made her way.

The two men watched her walk out, her every step taking their breath away. Mike felt Alessandro had seen enough. "Alright, buddy, that's good. Sit, we have business to discuss," he declared.

Alessandro returned to his seat. "Yes, Mike, I discerned that much. What can I do for you?"

"First, Alessandro, we are gentlemen, professionals, aren't we? Family is off limits."

"But, of course, Mike. That is what differentiates us from the barbarians,"

Mike's eyes narrowed, turning slightly dark—a look no one wanted to see, especially Alessandro. "Then recall your man, or I can assure you that you have already taken your last breath."

Alessandro turned to see one of his bodyguards following Christina to the restroom. He quickly raised his hand and snapped his fingers. Almost instinctively, the man returned to a table behind the two men.

"That's better. Thank you, Alessandro."

"Of course, Mike. My man meant nothing by it, I can assure you. Now, you were saying something about business. What can I do for you?"

"You have a case. One that you're set to deliver in Milan tomorrow. I need that case."

Alessandro scoffed at the request. "Mike, what does the United States want with such a trivial item? I believe you might be mistaken here. Truly, it is not worth the mighty Mike McHaskell's time for such an insignificant article."

"That might be, but I need it all the same," Mike answered, unfazed by the scoff.

Alessandro carefully weighed his words, knowing the stakes could not be any higher for him. "Mike, there must be some mistake. Please call Markus. Truly, it is of no importance to your country. I would tell you if it were otherwise. After all, we are friends."

"I wouldn't call us friends, Alessandro, not exactly. Look, I know you're contracted for $10 million; how about I double it to 20? Does that make you feel better about not giving to the other guy?"

Alessandro's face betrayed his inner turmoil. $20 million was way too much for such an item. "Mike, that is more than generous, and I would take it, I truly would. Alas, I have already entered into a contract with another buyer. You would not want me to go against my word, would you? I think not; remember, we are gentlemen."

Mike shook his head, "Gentlemen? Well, that's a fluid term, isn't it? Alessandro, we have a contract. The CIA gets the first right of refusal on any and all items that come into your possession. Are you telling me that you want to break that contract with the U.S.?"

"Of course not, Mike. You are my biggest and best customer. However, this particular item is for a new buyer of mine. We are testing the waters, and if it works out, they could quickly become a significant part of my business. Not as big, of course, as you, but substantial all the same. Mi dispiace, but I must pass on your offer."

This surprised Mike. *Alessandro is taking a pass?* he thought. "What do you mean a pass? Buddy, there is no pass with me. If we can't come to some sort of arrangement, then I'll need to get more 'creative' in my negotiation. Do you understand what I am saying?"

"Yes, I do. But, Mike, you do not understand. My new buyers... they are not gentlemen like us. In fact, they are more on the barbaric side of things."

"Barbaric side? Who are these buyers? And why would you associate yourself with people like that?"

"It is the Chinese, Mike, and because they have increased their game in the 'world' we occupy. China has money, lots of money. They strive to someday compete with the U.S., not only in the manufacturing arena but on the world stage in global domination."

"China? Alessandro, they cannot be trusted, believe me. Look, I'll up my offer to $25 million. Take it, brother; it's the last one you're gonna get."

"Fine, Mike, I accept. I only hope that my contact in Milan understands my dilemma. I shudder to think if he does not." Alessandro's face once again showed sadness, though Mike thought it looked more like terror, albeit not as much as a few moments ago when he gave his final warning.

At least I still hold some power, Mike thought. He said aloud, "Alessandro, you need to get out of bed with the Chinese. They are bad news, bro, bad news. I would say maybe even worse than the radicalized Islamic guys. At least with them, you know what they want. With the Chinese, who knows? This week, the U.S., next, Italy. Keep clear, man."

"Yes, well, here is your case. Thank you for your business." Alessandro handed him a small silver camera case. It was light, very light.

Jesus, $25 million for this? Mike thought. He quickly stashed it beside him so that when Christina returned, she wouldn't see it. "Hey, just out of curiosity, who is your contact in Milan? Is the guy Chinese?" he asked.

"I have never met the man before, but I hear tell he is someone *Big* in the Chinese government; they call him General. However, he is not in the military; at least, I do not believe he is."

This caught Mike's attention. "General?"

Alessandro answered, "Yes, General Feng Wu. He was to meet me at the opening of La Prima Sfilata tomorrow night. He is in town for the fashion show. However, now I believe our conversation might be a bit brief."

What a Waste:

After dinner, Mike and Christina returned to the Royal Windsor Suite. Mike tried to semi-explain the case in his hand, but Christina didn't push him on it. After finding out it wasn't for her, she cared little about it.

"Babe, I need to make a phone call; I will be right in," he said as they approached the car door.

"Okay, but don't be too long; we only have a few hours left to get the job done," she gave him a playful wink.

Mike almost jumped out of his clothes, forgetting about the conversation he needed to have with Markus.

"Alright, Stud, keep it in your pants. See you in a bit." Christina opened the door and then was out of sight.

Mike found a quiet place to call Markus. "Brother, we have a problem..."

The two men argued momentarily before Markus pulled the "I am your Boss" card. "I knew Mike, of course, I knew. Alessandro is selling to the Chinese."

"Do you know the best part? Who his contact in Milan?"

Markus sat back in his chair; he did know but hoped Mike wouldn't find out. "No, I guess I was left in the dark about that. Who is it, Mike?" he asked.

A smile crossed Mike's face when he uttered the words, "General Feng Wu. That bastard is out in public. You know what that means, don't you, brother?"

Among his other responsibilities, Markus's role as Director of the CIA required him to avoid sparking international incidents. Assassinating General Wu, the Chinese Minister of State Security, would undoubtedly qualify as such. Yet, Markus also knew Wu had a hand in the death of Agent Lai Zhou. Add to that, Mike and the General had, let's say, a checkered past. The Director anticipated difficulties in reining in his operative.

With these factors in mind, Markus weighed his options before speaking. "Mike, yes, I understand the implications." He paused, reflecting on the potential global and personal fallout of such a decision. He was deeply fond of Mike's family—the McHaskells—and cherished his role as "Uncle Markus" to the family's children. This bond gave him a sense of belonging and love that he lacked in his own personal life. These relationships were a significant part of Markus's life, and he feared that making the wrong decision could jeopardize these connections.

The Director grappled with these thoughts as he came to a decision. It was a choice that might alter his relationship with Mike and potentially estrange him from the family he held dear. But as Director of the CIA, Markus understood that difficult decisions came with the territory, decisions that he would have to live with. In this case, he concluded that the risks outweighed the benefits. "No, General Wu will be spared—at least for now."

Mike was seething with rage, struggling to maintain even a modicum of composure. "Markus, you've got to be fucking kidding me! That bastard is responsible for so many deaths. Not just Lai, who you know I need to avenge, but also those soldiers in Afghanistan. Damn it, man, don't you remember those guys? And the oath we took that night, swearing we'd get even with that guy someday? Well, our chance is right here, right now in Milan. And I'm going to take it."

"Mike, did you hear yourself just now? You said 'avenge.' Mike, we don't avenge anyone. We follow orders." Markus knew this was a losing battle and needed to resolve it now. "Listen, I hear you. And yes, the General needs to pay. So, if you want to... then do it. However, you have Christina with you, and she needs to be protected."

Mike listened as the Director shuffled through papers on his desk, staying silent to hear the man out.

The Director continued, "The President has us stretched thin right now. I don't have many assets to help you. There is one person, though, Caruso. He could at least keep watch over Christina. If you're going to do this, you need to promise me your bloodlust won't put her in harm's way. Mike, I need to hear the actual words from you."

"Come on, Markus, you know Christina is my world. I would never put her in danger. Of course, I won't."

"Hmm-hmm, sure, Mike. I seem to remember a trip to Japan." Markus caught himself mid-sentence. That was too much. Mike and Christina, even after a few years, still hadn't come to terms with the loss of their child. He continued, "Yes, brother, I know you will keep her safe. I have another person I can send you. It just might take a day or so."

"Thanks, Markus. I know this was unexpected, but he's out of China. That never happens, not since Afghanistan, anyway. Thanks, brother, really, thanks."

"Don't thank me, Mike. If this goes the wrong way, it could put us both behind bars or worse."

Mike had another issue to discuss with Markus: the potential fallout when Alessandro informed the General that the case was lost and the deal canceled.

"Hmm," Markus paused, reflecting on the situation. "Here's the deal: Alessandro made his choice. If he's now working with the Chinese, he's of no use to us anymore. He crafted his fate; now, he must embrace it."

Mike found Markus's stance harsh. *That's cold, very cold,* he thought. "Okay, Boss, it's your call."

The Director was about to hang up the phone, but Mike broke the silence before he could do so.

"Wait, Markus. What do you want me to do with this case? Drop it off at the embassy?"

"Oh yeah, I almost forgot. Good, I knew you would get it. Just trash it; we don't need it."

"Trash it? Dude, $25 mil, and you say just trash it? What's in it anyway?" Mike shook the case as he was speaking.

"$25 MILLION! Mike, I said 15 tops, not a penny more. What the hell, man!"

"Oh yeah..." Mike trailed off.

"Jesus, Michael! That's coming out of your end. I have Congress breathing all over me about our spending. My God, you just…"

"It's cool, brother. I can cover it. Really though, what's in it?" Mike asked again.

"Ah, nothing we can use. It's a formula for jet fuel. It boosts the efficiency by three percent. We already have it. I just didn't want the Chinese to get it. No big deal."

Mike entered the rail cabin; Christina was stretched out across the bed, watching her iPad. She looked so beautiful. He loved her so much. She glanced up and smiled at him.

"Hey, you were gone a while. Everything okay?" she asked.

"Of course, Babe, everything is fine now," he said as he opened the window.

Christina couldn't help but ask, "What are you doing?" Before she finished her words, the case in Mike's right hand was on its way to the bottom of a 4,000-foot ravine deep in the heart of the Alps.

"Christina, if I ever give you trouble about your spending again, just remind me of that case. I promise I will leave you alone."

The Emporer Suite:

The following day, Christina awoke to find Mike sitting on a chair, watching her sleep. His lips curved into a larger-than-life smile. She returned a smile of her own. They just stared at each other, not saying a word because none were needed. People who knew the couple would say they shared one mind and could communicate with simple eye gestures or small nods. And this might have been true.

Mike's relationships with each of his wives were markedly different. Claire was his rock and his soulmate, his true partner in life. She was everything that kept him grounded and balanced. Claire was the glue that kept the McHaskells together, all the McHaskells.

Parker was his energizer and physical challenger. They sparred mentally as well as physically; She acted as his social conscience, a 'normal' one, which he lacked. With her, he was developing a sort of moral compass.

Bailey, on the other hand, was his equal in a unique sense. They shared killer instincts, not in the conventional, literal sense like Mike, but in her ability to sense corporate blood in the water, launch the kill shot, and return to her home life without a second thought. Bailey had a knack for spotting hidden gems amidst financial ruins. She would take failing companies, leverage their financial struggles to attack, and dismantle them for parts or revamp the mismanaged assets to sell them off at a substantial profit. Her only objective, the same as Mike, was to make the world better for her family.

Then, there was Elena, with whom Mike openly shared his professional life. He liked to think that she was the only one who truly understood the intricacies of their work together. Elena and Mike were cut from the same cloth.

But his Christina was different from all the others. She and Mike shared one heart and one soul. She was his life, his best friend, and his most valuable treasure. Every time she entered a room, she took his breath away. Life without her was unimaginable, something he couldn't even begin to fathom. So when Markus reminded him that Christina could be put in danger, Mike had a brief but real physical pain in his heart. He would never do anything to jeopardize his 'love' again.

Christina gently asked, "How long have you been awake?"

Mike answered, "A bit. I enjoy watching you sleep. So peaceful."

"You could have woken me up. You know, how I like to be…" She stretched and yawned, her naked body covered from the waist down. "What time is it?"

"It's almost four. We pull into the station in an hour. I wanted to let you sleep."

"Four? What? How could you let me sleep that long? Gosh, Mike, I need to get this place packed up…"

"Babe, you needed rest. I mean, we were up all night again. And you really didn't get any sleep the night before, either. Besides, I have people coming in to pack us up and take our stuff to the hotel in thirty minutes. Just relax, my Queen."

"Thirty minutes, you say... Hmm, then why don't you come join me for a few of them?" She playfully held the sheets up off the rest of her body and motioned for him to join her.

Mike's "smile" grew even larger.

The couple arrived at Hotel Principe di Milan around six pm that night. The Principe was one of Milan's most extravagant and luxurious hotels. Reservations were nearly impossible to secure, but that was only for outsiders to the exclusive club the McHaskells now found themselves members of. This was primarily thanks to Bailey, who, in her short time running the family business, had significantly increased the household's wealth. Her keen intellect for investments and an almost 'visionary' ability to predict market trends had doubled the family's fortune in just eighteen months, a feat that did not go unnoticed.

Christina fully embraced the 'windfall' and "upped" her game in the fashion world. This, combined with the tickets Markus had given them, was the primary reason (as far as they knew) that the couple was staying in the Emporer Suite at the hotel.

Regarding fashion, the following day marked the beginning of the renowned Milan Fashion Week. Aware of Christina's passion for style, Mike, with his newest wife Bailey's assistance, asserted their 'influence' to secure tickets for the couple to attend all events, from the opening night ceremonies to the closing evening festivities four days later. Christina would have the opportunity to purchase whatever she desired to wear for each event. At the same time, Mike would stand by and watch his wife excel in her element.

That was the plan, anyway. However, Mike now found himself on a Mission—a Mission he alone had decided was necessary.

The Exterior of the Hotel Principe di Milan looked like a castle, and the interior illuminated as though only royalty was inside. The hotel's interior was sheer elegance, and the Emporer Suite, full of history and extravagance, would be perfect for Christina.

"Mike, get a load of this place; oh my gosh, it's amazing!" Christina gazed at the walls, the floors, the stairs. She spun around, taking in the incredible sights surrounding them.

"Hello Christina, Mike. It's good to see you both," the words were spoken by a familiar and very welcome voice.

Christina immediately burst out, "Elena! Oh my Gosh! Elena! I didn't know you were gonna be here! This is so awesome!" The two women embraced while Christina again squealed, "Mike, Elena is here! Isn't that great!"

"Hello Elena, Yes, it's nice to see you," Mike replied.

The two stood there, motionless, as if an invisible force held them back from acting like a husband and wife who hadn't seen each other in a while. Christina instantly took note, "Well, hug you two, my gosh. Brrr...." She pretended like it was cold and hugged herself to keep warm.

"Of course, hello, Mike." Elena offered her arms in an embrace; Mike returned the gesture.

"That's better," Christina said with a smile. "Hey, Elena, we're in the Emporer Suite. Grab your stuff; I'm dying to see it."

Elena spoke up, "Actually, Christina, I'm in room 304." She looked at Mike and continued, "I thought since it's your anniversary, I should get my own room."

"Nonsense! Room 304, you said?" Christina marched to the registration desk and, in flawless Italian, declared, "Sir, my sister will stay in our room. I would like her bags brought up from room 304. Grazie." She then turned back to Mike and Elena, "See, all sorted. Your stuff will be moved. Now, let's go." The whirlwind that was Christina glided toward the elevators before they could even respond.

The only sound was Elena's questioning remark, "She speaks Italian?"

"Yeah, long story," Mike replied.

The trio entered what would be their home for the next five days. Christina, who had been chatting the entire way up in the private elevator, was finally speechless. Although they would never admit it, the silence was a welcome respite for Mike and Elena. Christina had been stuck on one track, talking non-stop about the fun she anticipated the three of them having together during the week.

The Emporer suite, modeled after an ancient Roman palace, epitomized luxury and extravagance unmatched by any other. At its heart was a sunken living room, an expansive space trimmed with rich, plush sofas that looked as though they were taken straight from a scene set two thousand years ago. The furniture, while maintaining an antique aesthetic, was upholstered with the most lavish fabrics known to man, each piece feeling like a cloud to the touch.

On either side of the living room were two grand bedrooms, each a sanctuary of comfort and elegance in its own right. Large and inviting beds were dressed in the finest linens that seemed to call out to its occupants, promising a night of blissful rest. Each was paired with its own private bathroom, a marvel of modern luxury blended seamlessly with classic Roman architecture. The floors were covered with intricate mosaics, the walls etched with scenes of ancient Rome, bringing history to life.

It was a marriage of past and present, a place where one could live like an Emperor while still enjoying the conveniences of modern life.

The silence didn't last long, however. Once Christina regained her bearings, she was off again. "Oh my God, this place is awesome!" she exclaimed as she dashed into one of the bedrooms. Once inside, she called out to Mike, "Hey, come in here! You have to check out this bed... Ooooo, it's going to see so much action tonight."

Mike chuckled at the remark. Elena, watching his face, decided to break the ice between them. "Mike, if you would like me to go down to the other room, I will. I didn't mean to mess up your time with Christina."

He replied, "No, Elena, you stay. Of course, you stay. You're my wife, too. Really, I've missed you, and I'm happy you're here."

"Are you, Mike? Really? I think we need to have a talk about... You know... things."

Mike replied in the only way he could, "Yes, we do, Elena. I would like that."

Later that night, after a dinner that could only be described as "tense," featuring primarily a one-sided conversation with only Christina doing the talking, the trio made their way back to the suite. Mike, clearly exhausted, expressed his desire to head straight to bed. Christina, changing her clothes, waited for him to finish his shower. It was unusual for her; typically, she'd join him, but Mike, breaking from his usual habit, chose to shower alone. Christina wasn't too surprised, given how poorly she felt dinner had gone. The tension wasn't between her and Mike, but the atmosphere between Mike and Elena was more strained than she had anticipated. Resolving to address the situation, Christina decided to take charge. She headed to Elena's bedroom, determined to mend what she could.

There was a gentle rap at the door, and Christina asked, "Hey, can I come in?"

Elena answered, "Of course, Sweetheart."

"I wanted to talk to you about everything. Elena, I don't know what to do here. Seeing you and Mike like this, well, it's heartbreaking. What can I do to help?"

Elena knew this conversation was coming. All night, Christina had been trying to reach some kind of understanding with the couple, but neither would budge. She responded, "Honey, honestly, I don't think there's much you can do. Sadly, I think Mike and I might be over, or at least almost. I wish it weren't the case, but as you can clearly see from tonight's events, it just might be."

"Please, Elena, don't give up. I know we haven't always seen eye to eye, but we've come a long way. Mike loves you, and I think you love him too. Give it another chance. Yeah, this long-distance crap is tough, but we've got to make it work. You can't just walk away from us, Elena. You just can't."

Last year, just before Mike Jr. was born, Christina and Elena had a heart-to-heart about their marriage to Mike. Christina opened up, sharing her frustrations about the whole situation and her true feelings about Elena and Mike. She expressed her concern that Elena didn't take the marriage seriously and seemed to treat the family like a backup plan. Elena, surprised by the conversation, clarified her position. She was, in fact, deeply in love with the family and reassured her of her commitment. After this exchange, the two women finally found common ground, with Christina accepting Elena's promise to be more present in the future. However, as Elena's work obligations increased, she became absent again, but this time, she made a conscious effort to keep Christina in the know as much as possible.

Things started to improve, but eventually, Mike and Elena began drifting apart again. Days turned into weeks, and weeks into months, until it reached a point where Mike and Elena hadn't seen each other for nearly a year.

"Really, Honey, I haven't been with Mike since the month Jr was born. We have just drifted apart. I am not sure we can make it work." Elena's eyes displayed her emotions. She was distraught, upset, and on the verge of tears.

"Let's fix that. There's no reason to just give up. It's my anniversary week, and I want to make it special for our husband." Christina reached out for her hand. "Come with me. You and I can give Mike a night he will never forget. It will be good for both of you. For all of us."

Elena laughed, "Sweetheart, I know you might think I have experience in what you're suggesting, but I can assure you, I do not. I've never..."

Christina interrupted her mid-sentence, "Well, neither have I, not really anyway. But I am willing to, I don't know... I guess try? Is that something you might be interested in? I mean, maybe not sleep together, just to show Mike a really good night, that's all. Besides, I know you still love him. Come on, Elena, let's make this work."

Her smile was so captivating. How could Elena have said no? The two held hands, took a deep breath, and entered their husband's bedroom. That night would be one of many firsts and, hopefully, a new beginning for a struggling marriage.

Have a Pleasant Flight Home:

Two men stood solemnly over a body that once brimmed with life, shrouded in the shadows of ancient tunnels beneath Milan. These subterranean passageways, carved long ago by the Romans, had served as both a refuge and a strategic defense point for the city. They were an architectural marvel designed to protect not only the citizens but also the invaluable assets of the Roman Empire during its turbulent final days. As the Huns, led by the notorious Attila, launched their assaults from the far reaches of Asia, these caverns provided a crucial sanctuary. The air was thick with history, each stone echoing tales of resilience and survival from an era when the world trembled under the march of the great Attila the Hun.

Echoing through were the remnants of history's whispers, punctuated just moments ago by the final screams of a man. He had been clad in a pristine white suit, now marred with crimson stains. Clinging to his lapel was the remains of a flower, a white gardenia, its purity contrasting starkly with the scene of despair.

One of the "executioners" meticulously cleaned his "tools," each glistening under the dim light as he placed them back into their designated slots in a leather pouch. They were reminiscent of a butcher's set, varied in size and purpose, each having played its part. As he finished the last of the cleaning, he carefully rolled up the toolkit and turned his attention to the other man beside him. With a calm, measured tone, he remarked, "You see, Mr.

Wang, there's an art to making anyone speak. It's all about finding the right leverage." The words hung heavily in the air, echoing the grim reality of the situation.

"Yes, Inspector Tseng, I never doubted you would recover the information the General requested. You are a master at this, Sir," replied Wang, his voice carrying a mix of respect and unease.

Inspector Tseng gave a slight nod, his expression unchanging. "Your words are so kind, Mr. Wang, but truly, it was effortless. Absolutely effortless. You see, individuals like Mr. Vitali present little to no challenges. They lack a certain... constitution, shall we say. Fragile in spirit, quickly undone with the proper 'persuasion.'" His tone was matter-of-fact, betraying no hint of pride or discomfort at the task he had just completed.

"Now, I must take my leave. Please, attend to this mess, will you?" The Inspector gestured towards the lifeless body slumped over a chair. Mr. Wang nodded in understanding. The Inspector continued, "Excellent, I appreciate your efforts, my friend. I shall convey this information to the General. Until our paths cross once more, Mr. Wang."

The two men shared a slight bow, a gesture of mutual respect in their grim line of work. Inspector Zhu Tseng then turned and opened an ancient wooden door to his right. He walked down a long corridor, its walls a patchwork of stone and brick, his footfalls echoing with each step he took. As he neared the end of the corridor, bright sunlight beamed down, momentarily blinding him as he approached the exit. Adjusting to the light, he stepped out and entered a black town car waiting for him. The driver acknowledged him with a nod. They sped off, vanishing into the daylight and leaving behind the sinister whispers that lingered in the shadowy depths of that underground chamber.

A deep and ominous voice broke the silence, "I trust you were successful, Inspector?"

"Naturally, General Wu. He proved most cooperative, Sir." Inspector Zhu Tseng smoothly retrieved a piece of paper from the inside of his black suit jacket and handed it to the General. His expression was one of veiled triumph, reflecting his pride in successfully extracting the information the General desired. "I believe you recognize this individual, General," he said, the underlying satisfaction evident in his voice, knowing the name on the paper belonged to a man they both wanted, "eliminated."

General Feng Wu, the Chinese Minister of State Security, slowly read the name. A malevolent smile crept across his lips, his right hand delicately tracing the scar that journeyed from where his right eye once was to his cheek, now hidden beneath a black eyepatch. "Yes, Inspector," he began, his voice dripping with venomous anticipation, "I do believe today is going to be a splendid day, indeed. Very splendid." His laughter, icy and sinister, filled the vehicle, a sound so chilling it could unsettle even the most hardened of souls. "Now, my dear Inspector, my man will take you to the airport. Have a pleasant flight home."

"Yes, General. And good 'hunting' to you, Sir."

I Did As You Asked:

The following morning, Christina was on the phone, navigating a conversation with her sister. Mike and Elena had risen early and were already out of the room, giving her a moment of privacy. With a busy day ahead, Christina was keen to wrap up the call quickly so she could start getting ready.

"Yes, Claire, I did as you asked. Mike and Elena are back on 'track,'" Christina stated as she continued highlighting the night's events.

As she delved into the "vivid" details, she knew these were topics her sister would find less than appealing. It was a familiar game between them, a dynamic stretching back to their childhood – Claire, the prim and proper, versus Christina, the complete opposite of her sister.

Claire responded with a mix of bewilderment and practicality, "Well, I certainly didn't suggest you do that, Christina, and I didn't need to hear all the details either, I might add. But okay then,.... I guess. So, how is everything else? Like your hotel room, and oh, how's the coffee? I bet it's great." Her tone shifted, steering the conversation towards safer, more mundane topics.

Christina responded, still with amusement over Claire's embarrassment, "Everything's great. But how are my babies? I miss them so much. Little Mikey? And the others?"

Claire assured, "They're all wonderful and miss you and their daddy too. I'll send over some photos."

"Of course, you will. Hey Claire, sorry, but I have to run. Mike's coming back in. Your plan is working perfectly; I'll keep you updated." She couldn't help but smile as she playfully added, "In all ways updated," followed by a soft laugh.

"Oh gosh, goodbye, Christina. Have a nice trip," Claire replied, a mixture of amusement and exasperation in her voice as she shook her head and hung up the phone.

"Good morning, Gorgeous," Mike announced as he walked in, holding a hot cup of coffee and a pastry.

"Awesome, thank you, Honey," Christina replied, swiftly grabbing and devouring the pastry.

Mike watched in amusement. "Babe, you should chew it before swallowing," he laughed.

"Oh my God, I am so hungry I could eat my shoes, and I love my Jimmy's," she replied, glancing at his empty hands. "That's all you brought me? One measly little Danish? What the hell?" Her tone was half-joking, half-serious, a playful scowl crossing her face.

"Sorry, Babe, I didn't know. I could..." Mike started, but Christina was quick to respond.

"No, Mike, it's fine. Now, I need to get ready. We need to be at the showroom no later than noon."

"Yeah, about that, Honey..." he started, his eyes shifting towards the floor, clearly searching for a way out of the commitment. However, Christina was stubborn and not in the mood for any excuses.

"Mike, you promised! Do you know how hard it was to get a private showing from The Maestro? The work Bailey put in? All the paperwork and arrangements? It would have been easier to get into Fort Knox than to see his workshop. And you promised you'd come with me."

"I know, Sexy. Of course, I will go with," Mike conceded, knowing the argument was already lost. Still, he needed to meet with his contact and figure out his new mission, a task that was starting to consume his mind. He had enough on his plate with Elena, Christina, and now the General.

"Good. Now, I need to shower. Could you please leave so I can get ready?" Christina jumped out of bed and headed towards the bathroom. Mike couldn't help but watch her; unlike him and Elena, Christina was still naked, her nightgown lying on the floor where Mike had removed it the night before.

"Hey, I could help you in there, just a suggestion," he offered playfully.

Christina laughed, "Yeah, right, 'help.' I think I can wash my own boobs, thank you. Now, please go; I'll be ready in an hour."

Along with the coveted invitation to the fashion show, Bailey had managed a remarkable feat – securing an exclusive visit for Christina and Mike to see the renowned Lorenzo Cavallaro, Italy's most elusive and passionate fashion designer. Known as "The Grandiose Maestro." Cavallaro was the star attraction at this year's show. His eagerly awaited new collection, "Eredità del Mito (Mythos Legacy)," was shrouded in mystery. No one outside his tight-knit inner circle had any inkling of the collection's contents or aesthetic direction.

His showroom, nestled within a historic palazzo in Milan, was a veritable fortress of secrecy. Press members, patrons, and even government officials were not only denied entry but also barred from peeking through the meticulously covered windows. This level of security only heightened the anticipation and intrigue surrounding Cavallaro's latest creations, making the exclusive access Bailey had secured all the more enviable.

This morning, Christina needed to add one more invite to the list, Elena. When she called to update Claire, the two worked out the request. Bailey was on the phone with the "Maestro" moments later.

While working at Gold, Smith, and Wallinsky, Bailey McHaskell, then Bailey Banasiński, first crossed paths with the then-unknown designer Lorenzo Cavallaro, known in those days by his birth name Luca Moretti. Moretti, brimming with innovative designs and a fiery spirit, was held back only by a lack of funds. Their paths converged in New York at a venture capital summit, where they struck up a conversation that would change both their lives.

Moretti was instantly captivated by Bailey's sharp intellect—a reaction shared by many who met her. He recognized in her the catalyst that could launch his dreams into reality. With her help and the backing of her firm, Luca Moretti transformed into Lorenzo Cavallaro, The Grandiose Maestro of Fashion. This metamorphosis was just one of the many feathers in Bailey's professional cap.

She was a financial powerhouse with a Midas touch that seemed to turn the most modest of opportunities into gleaming successes. Bailey had an uncanny ability to find a diamond in the rough, a rare talent in the high-stakes realm of finance and venture capital. Her involvement in Cavallaro's rise to fame was a testament to this unique gift, marking her as a formidable figure in the business world.

Mike followed Christina to the bathroom door, wanting to express his gratitude for her role in reconciling him and Elena. "You two just needed to get out of your heads, that's all. It was no big deal. I'm glad I could help," She responded casually, brushing off the seriousness of her intervention.

"Yeah, but Honey, I still feel I need to thank you. Plus... last night was truly one of the best nights of my life. Not that any night with you isn't," Mike said, his smile broadening as he playfully raised his eyebrows suggestively at her. His expression was a blend of mischief and genuine gratitude for the most memorable of nights they had shared.

Christina responded with a wink and a smile mirroring his. "You should go and seal the deal. Just talk to her, Mike, and keep the baby conversation out of it. I mean it. Elena has made her decision, and now you must deal with it. Go to her, Honey; I'll see you in a bit."

Mike walked into the living area of the hotel suite, finding Elena seated at the table, engrossed in the newspaper. In front of her was a Danish, and she held a cup of coffee in her right hand.

"Hey," he greeted. "Christina is getting ready. I couldn't get out of the showroom bullshit today. That sucks." His tone carried a hint of frustration, though it was clear that his mind was on something more than just the showroom visit.

Elena picked up on his discomfort, recognizing the familiar pattern of Mike becoming withdrawn around her. Sensing the need to break the practice, she addressed the elephant in the room.

"So, what's the real reason you're upset, Mike? You usually love watching Christina flaunt her figure in those daring outfits. And that designer, I hear, specializes in just that—minimal fabric, maximum style." Her tone was lightly teasing, an attempt to ease the tension and encourage a more open conversation.

"I think we both understand what I'm struggling with. Last night was incredible; truly, Elena, it was. And I hope it marked the beginning of a new chapter for us. But we can't ignore the fact that we let things slide too far, for too long, last time. I don't want to see that happen again. I guess what I'm trying to say is, I'm afraid I might mess things up between us again." He gestured between them, emphasizing 'us.' "It scares me, Elena."

"It wasn't just your fault, Mike. I am as much to blame. I knew your expectations when we got married, and I should have been clearer about mine. You knew I wanted to return to Europe and that children would complicate things."

She paused, sensing the conversation drifting back toward their unresolved issues from the past year. Choosing a different path, she continued, "How about this: let's just have a nice week and take things one step at a time. I really do love you, Mike, and I want this to work. Can we agree to start fresh, please?"

Mike nodded in agreement, "Yes, Honey, I think that would be great."

Palazzo dei Sogni:

Entering the renowned Palazzo dei Sogni (The Palace of Dreams), Lorenzo Cavallaro's brand-new, state-of-the-art flagship showroom, the trio was immediately struck by its magnificence. Just a month prior, Cavallaro's partnership had undergone a significant change when Gold, Smith, and Wallinsky sold their stakes, transferring half of the company's shares to a new investor. This entity, preferring to operate from the shadows, stood at the forefront to reap the benefits of Lorenzo's latest collection—a bold initiative destined to enchant the fashion industry. With the formation of this new alliance, the acquisition of this magnificent showroom was made possible.

Stepping through the dramatic wrought-iron gate, the historic Palazzo, restored to opulent grandeur, unfolded before them. Frescoed ceilings, gilded moldings, and marble floors that echoed their footsteps welcomed them into a world of luxurious fantasy.

The cobblestone courtyard they crossed was embellished with oversized sculptures, each dressed in Cavallaro's most extravagant creations, showcasing his wild imagination and flair for the dramatic.

The interior of the Palazzo was nothing short of a theatrical masterpiece. Each room was its own distinct universe: one a jungle draped in emerald velvet gowns and adorned with leopard-print accessories; another, a boudoir swathed in crimson silk, sparkling with crystals. Secret passageways led to astonishing discoveries—a mirrored catwalk here, a hidden garden of floral-inspired dresses there.

Cutting-edge technology was interwoven with the lavish décor. Interactive displays narrated Cavallaro's creative journey, while holographic projections of runway shows brought his visions to life. In a corner, AI stylists analyzed visitors, suggesting outfits that seemed custom-made for each person.

This was more than just a showroom; it was an immersive expedition into the heart of Cavallaro's genius, a fusion of fashion and fantasy where artistry and apparel melded into a breathtaking experience.

Of course, Christina was ecstatic, like a kid in a candy store. Everything in the Palazzo dei Sogni seemed as if it had been custom-tailored to fulfill her every desire. The displays, the fabrics, the cuts—all spoke directly to her fashion-forward heart.

Mike, however, wasn't as taken. To him, many of the displays bordered on being too risqué. This edgy quality was something Christina adored in The Maestro's designs, but for Mike, it was a bit over the top. The fabrics, though almost magical in their drape and flow, left little to the imagination, treading a fine line between daring and way too revealing—a line a bit too far for his comfort.

Lorenzo Cavallaro, the mastermind behind these creations, revered the female form, viewing it as the epitome of beauty, something to be celebrated rather than concealed. His designs, aggressive and unapologetic, were fully embraced by the fashion world. This acclaim seemed only to bolster his creativity, pushing boundaries further with each collection, fueling his belief in showcasing rather than hiding the natural beauty of the body. His success in the industry was undeniable, each piece a forceful statement against convention, constantly testing the limits of fashion and decency.

As Mike and Elena observed Christina, utterly lost in her version of heaven, a woman approached them. "Hello, you must be the McHaskells," she greeted with a warm smile. "My name is Ambrosia Ambrosetti. I am Mr. Cavallaro's assistant and will be your guide at this showing."

"Hello, Ambrosia," Mike replied, his voice carrying a somewhat forced-polite tone.

Elena, meanwhile, simply nodded in acknowledgment, her attention unwaveringly fixed on Christina. She didn't utter a word, her eyes following Christina's every move, not missing a beat.

While Christina was getting ready this morning, Mike and Elena took the opportunity to discuss their plans without the heat of an argument. Mike laid out his need for Elena to keep a watchful eye on Christina while he devised his strategy for dealing with General Feng Wu. Elena, fully grasping the gravity of the situation and aware that the Chinese didn't consider family off-limits, agreed readily. However, she was adamant about being a part of the Mission once Mike finalized the specifics.

As the Chief of Station in Europe, Elena benefited from her own security detail—two officers tasked with shadowing her wherever she went. These Agents were discreet, especially when Mike was present, knowing his preference for privacy with his wife. Yet, they were always close at hand, ready to resume their protective duties the moment he was out of sight, ensuring the safety of the Chief at all times.

Mike continued, "Your English is great. Did you study in the States?"

"Yes, well, I'm American. Really, my name is Scarlett Jenson. Mr. Cavallaro believed that I needed an 'upgrade,'" she replied with a hint of amusement in her voice. "If you would follow me, I will take you to your private showroom."

Mike murmured to Elena as Scarlett walked ahead, "All bullshit. I can't wait to meet this guy."

Elena hummed in response, "Mmm-hmm."

Today was set for a private live showing of dresses Christina had meticulously picked out. But these weren't just for her. She had thoughtfully included selections for Claire, Parker, Bailey, and, unbeknownst to her, Elena. Christina had taken the initiative to send in every woman's sizes and had engaged with Cavallaro's AI system to design online, expressing her preferences in colors. She had also arranged for most of the items to be shipped back to Texas, save for the ones she planned to wear in Milan for the show.

Each dress would be showcased by a model closely matching each of the McHaskell women. The event would start with Claire, whose dress required extra consideration due to her "unique" taste, a concept Christina often found "ridiculous." However, Mike's complete approval was necessary before any dress could be deemed suitable for his Claire to wear.

"If you would please have a seat, the first showing will begin soon," Ambrosia spoke with a polite nod, then slipped behind the runway to the model staging area.

"Jesus, get a load of this place. Christina, how much are these things? And do I even want to know?" Elena finally broke her silence. This was the first time she had spoken since they left the hotel.

Christina began to worry, wondering if Elena was upset with her. They hadn't discussed what had happened the previous night, and Christina was anxious that she might have crossed a line. *Maybe Elena isn't as thrilled about the events as I am.* She thought.

She replied, "Well, yes, they are kind of expensive, but they're worth it. You'll see, trust me."

The first model stepped out and made her way down the runway toward the awaiting patrons. Mike couldn't take his eyes off the woman. "Damn, she looks just like Claire. Where did they find this girl?" he exclaimed.

Christina merely smiled at his remark, while Elena remained unimpressed. "No, she doesn't, not at all. You're just thinking with your..." She gave Mike a once-over before continuing, "...Yeah, that."

Mike's eyes scrutinized the gown. "Babe, there's no way Claire is going to wear that. I promise you, she won't. Although, I wouldn't mind it, not at all. I can only imagine her in it. But really, Honey, she won't, and I think you know that."

Christina responded confidently, "Yes, she will. It's for Bailey's thing next month. Trust me, I'll get her to wear it. That's if she isn't already showing again. That woman, sheesh."

It was time for Mike to leave; he had a meeting with Agent Caruso and was already running late. He gave Elena a nod, noticing Christina's eyes were still fixed on the model parading in front of them.

Elena leaned in, whispering into Christina's ear, "Hey, let's cut Mike loose. He's only going to get more upset and bossy when your outfits come out. Based on what you picked for Claire here, which I'm sure would be considered 'very conservative' compared to what you picked for yourself," she sarcastically gestured toward the dress, "then he'll have a fit. Better you just surprise him with it. What could he do then? Nothing really."

Christina nodded in agreement, then turned to him. "Honey, I know this isn't your thing. I saw you eyeing that beer garden when we drove up. Why don't you go and get us a table? We'll come over for lunch when we're done here."

"Wow, thanks, Babe. I'll see you both in a bit." Mike was already out the door before finishing his sentence. Elena chuckled softly, and Christina shook her head, smiling.

"Good idea, Elena," she remarked.

"Yep, now we can relax," Elena responded, settling in to enjoy the show.

The next model wasn't ready, causing a brief pause. Elena seized the opportunity to ask Christina a few questions.

"So, Claire's pregnant again?"

Christina, shaking her head, somewhat revolted, confirmed, "Yeah, she's on track for her '7.' This will be number 4 already."

"Wow, that was quick," Elena remarked, choosing her words thoughtfully before adding, "I noticed last night that Mike seemed quite determined. It appeared you were his main focus, his final destination."

Christina's face flushed with embarrassment, her lips twisting into a lopsided frown. "Gosh, I'm sorry about that, Elena. Yes, we're trying for another too. We just decided on this trip—well, actually, Mike decided and

I agreed. Sorry, you know how he is. He thinks he has a duty to 'fulfill.' I'll remind him to be more considerate of you."

"Oohhh, don't do that on my account. I could do without that—mess. I was just wondering why he was trying so hard, especially since he's already slipped one past the goalie, that's all."

Christina didn't respond immediately, giving the impression that Elena's comments hadn't affected her. "I'm not sure I know what you're talking about," she finally replied.

"You don't? Hmm... Well, last night at dinner, you ate your entire meal, then half of mine, and all of Mike's baked potato. Then you had two desserts. When I was twenty-one, I can't remember many times that I didn't have a drink in my hand. However, you only had soda last night. And then there's today. In front of me, in my champagne bucket, is a bottle of Prosecco. In front of you is a bottle of sparkling apple cider. I wonder why that is then."

Christina sunk into her chair for a moment, realizing her secret was out. "Okay, yes, I am, but don't tell Mike. I want it to be a surprise," she confessed.

"Already? You two just decided, you said?" Elena probed further.

"No, I'm about six weeks along. I found out the day before we left Texas. Mike and I were at a horse auction about that long ago in San Antonio. Frank sent us down to look at a couple of 'Bull Horses.' A local ranch was selling off its breeding program, and Frank wanted the bloodline. Anyway, that night, Mike had one of his," she gestured with air quotes, "'accidents.' And here we are."

Elena looked at Christina thoughtfully. "Is that really what you wanted? I thought you were planning to run a marathon this year. And, wow, you're in the best shape I've ever seen you in. I mean, your body, Christina, it's just... Amazing."

Christina nodded, "Yes, that was the plan. But no, I'm happy about it. My idea is to have all my kids while I'm young. Then, I can do what I want later and still have the body for it. That's my plan, anyway. I am happy, really. I think I am, at least." Her voice wavered slightly as if she was convincing herself that it was indeed a good thing. Elena could sense the uncertainty.

"I think you're right, Christina. It's probably better to get it out of the way while you can still bounce back so quickly." She offered a supportive smile, trying to reassure her young ally.

The McHaskell women had agreed to refer to themselves as "Life Allies." Claire was adamant about avoiding the term "sister wives," seeking a descriptor for their interconnected lives that was both non-stereotypical and accurate for introductions. Deep down, they all recognized the profound depth of their bond, far transcending any simple label. Elena, in particular, held Christina in her heart not merely as a partner in their shared journey but as someone profoundly dear to her.

As the next model strutted onto the runway, it didn't take long for Elena to recognize who she was meant to be emulating.

The woman moved with the grace and confidence characteristic of a Latina, her body showcasing tantalizing curves. She had a bodacious upper half, with hips to match and a waist narrow enough for Mike to almost encircle with his hands. Her dress was a stunning midnight blue, backless and strapless, with a daring v-cut plunging down the front. Two sheer, thin strips of fabric ran down, providing minimal coverage and straining as if they might burst at any moment. The material created an illusion of coverage, but as the model moved, slight, nearly indiscernible glimpses of her skin were revealed. This dress left little to the imagination, boldly showcasing almost everything. The display was brief, but it revealed all that was intended – and perhaps a bit more.

Elena's eyes widened in awe as the dress was revealed, its magic undeniable. "Christina, I don't think I can wear that. It's gorgeous, but no offense," she said, turning to the model, "You are a very beautiful woman, but your figure is quite different from mine." She then gestured towards her chest. "Christina, there's no way that, will hold up against these," she stated, half-joking about the dress's ability to contain her "formations."

Christina chuckled as she sent the model away. "Of course, it will fit. And look where we are – if there's any issue, I'm sure it can be adjusted. But honestly, I'd leave it as is. It'll drive Mike wild!"

Elena paused, considering. "Yes, I'm sure it will," she mused, then added with a playful tone, "Sweetheart, if this is what my dress looks like, I can't even begin to imagine yours... Oh boy, our poor husband. Plus, there is the cost of these things. Really, I don't think I could afford them anyway."

Christina grinned. "Actually, it's not too over the top; at least, I don't think so. Though the color might be a bit much for him. He'll just have to deal with it." She then turned to Ambrosia. "You can wrap mine up. I trust the maestro's work completely."

Ambrosia nodded, "Of course, Mrs. McHaskell. Just a moment, and I'll bring out the last of the dresses. Finding someone as tall as your Parker was a challenge, especially with the show starting tomorrow. But I think we found the perfect fit for her. I'll be right back."

Christina laughed, brushing off Elena's concerns. "Elena, don't worry about the cost. Bailey has some kind of arrangement with Lorenzo. Anyway, you can totally afford it. You could buy this entire place if you just accepted your share of the dividends from Bailey. She mentioned you haven't cashed a single check. What gives?"

Elena sighed deeply. "Because that money isn't mine, Christina. It belongs to you, Claire, Parker, and Bailey. I haven't done anything to earn it."

Christina rolled her eyes. "Oh my God, not this again. Elena, you are family; that's what you've done to earn it. Just take the money. Your Paris apartment is cool, but let's be honest—it could be better, much better. Remember that old building we saw last year? You could renovate the top floor, make it something awesome."

Elena seemed to ignore her, instead focusing on the dresses around them. "But how much do these even cost?" she asked, gesturing to the various mannequins. "They look like they're at least $3,000 to $5,000 each. That's way beyond my budget." Her voice trailed off, yet her eyes lingered on the gowns, betraying a hint of longing despite her protests.

Christina noticed her reaction and, with another light laugh, clarified, "Uuumm, no. Elena, they're more in the range of €40,000 to €45,000. But think about it. Each piece is a one-off. There will never be another exactly like the ones made for you. Every dress in here is one of a kind. Totally worth it, if you ask me."

Elena's jaw nearly dropped. "EUROs? €45,000? Are you kidding me?" The shock in her voice was evident, her disbelief at the staggering price tag clear in her expression. "Oh my GOD!"

Biagio Caruso:

The Central Intelligence Agency, like many of its counterparts, operates on a "Trust, but verify." premise, a phrase famously coined by President Reagan in the 1980s. However, this approach has been a practice of the Agency for decades, long before the former President articulated it.

In World War I, Italy initially sided with the Triple Alliance alongside Germany and Austria. However, due to internal pressures and external incentives, Italy shifted allegiances in 1915, driven by territorial ambitions. They sought to expand their borders into Austria and Hungary, joining the Triple Entente (Allies) to achieve this goal.

Then came World War II. Under Benito Mussolini's Fascist regime, Italy's initial stance was neutrality. However, history repeated itself, and the country eventually sided with the Axis Powers, aligning with Germany. Following Mussolini's downfall, Italy officially joined the Allies, though the Italian response was not uniform. Some fought alongside the Germans, others against the German occupiers, while many remained neutral.

On April 4th, 1949, Italy became one of the founding members of the North Atlantic Treaty Organization (NATO). While the CIA welcomed this, it also approached it with skepticism. Italy's historical flip-flopping made the world's largest Intelligence Agency cautious. Hence, the Trust rule was established.

The Trust Rule: "We trust our Allies, but we verify." To implement this, required certain individuals to be covertly embedded in various Agencies of Allied Nations. Italy was no exception, and this is where Mr. Biagio Caruso's role became crucial. His Mission? Ensure that the trust was backed by solid verification.

Biagio Caruso, affectionately known as "Bigs" among his friends or "paisans," was born in Philadelphia, Pennsylvania, in 1983, the third youngest in a bustling household of eight brothers and sisters. In 1977, his parents, Silvio and Stella, had emigrated from Italy, seeking a better life for their family in the United States. His three eldest brothers, Giuseppe, Antonio, and Enzo, were born in Italy before their journey, and he and the rest of the Caruso siblings were born in the United States.

Years later, a mix of homesickness and his uncles' appeals prompted Silvio to consider returning to his ancestral homeland, this time with all of his children. Despite his lack of interest in the business, he had received a request to return to Naples to help manage the family's dairy farm. The property with a 180-head herd had been in the family lineage for generations and was in desperate need of Silvio's business management abilities as well as the free labor his wife and children would provide.

However, this plan faced opposition from his "Americanized" children, particularly the three oldest boys, who expressed no interest in uprooting their lives. Giuseppe, Antonio, and Enzo were old enough to live independently and chose to remain in the United States. The Caruso family embarked on their journey back across the Great Pond to Naples without the three eldest children.

On the day of departure, as Biagio watched the shoreline of New York disappear, he resolved to return to America, his country of birth. His parents spoke Italian as their first language, and all of the Caruso siblings spoke Italian and English fluently. Despite his familiarity with all things Italian, Italy felt foreign to him. To Biagio, Italy was a country marked by hardship and heartache and not the apparent sense of home and comfort it was to his father.

Tragically, during the first year after their return to Italy, his older brother Julius, who was only two years his senior, passed away from a childhood illness. The family often lamented that Julius died of a broken heart after leaving America behind. A sentiment that Biagio believed to be true. This conviction only strengthened his determination to return to the United States as soon as he had the opportunity. His time in Italy, overshadowed by the loss and the struggles of adjusting to a new life, left an indelible mark on Biagio, shaping his desires and future decisions.

After his return to the States, Biagio Caruso encountered a woman in 2001 at the University of New York in Albany who would significantly alter the course of his life. This meeting came just weeks after the tragic events of September 11th, a time when the Agency was urgently recruiting to fill positions globally. Experienced officers already embedded in foreign governments were being redeployed into a new, albeit familiar, arena: the world of counter-terrorism. This shift left a vacuum in many critical positions that needed urgent filling.

Chief Albert Walker Gray, responsible for this task, directed his team to find the nation's best and brightest. With relentless determination, his recruiters scoured college campuses nationwide, meticulously examining transcripts, notes, and any other intelligence at their disposal. During this exhaustive search, Margaret Hess, Senior Recruitment Officer, stumbled upon Biagio Caruso's file.

Biagio was an ideal candidate. He was intelligent, dynamic, bilingual in Italian and English, and possessed dual citizenship in the United States and Italy. His profile stood out as an exemplary fit for the Agency's needs. In him, they saw not just a potential Agent but a bridge between two nations in their Intelligence Networks.

The Agenzia Informazioni e Sicurezza (AIS), translated as the Internal Security and Information Agency, is Italy's equivalent of the CIA. However, compared to the CIA's singular structure, it operates with two distinct branches. The first branch, Agenzia Informazioni e Sicurezza Esterna (AISE), is responsible for foreign intelligence. To be frank, this branch was of less interest to the CIA, given that the U.S. already possessed extensive global intelligence capabilities.

The second branch, however, was of significant interest. The Sicurezza Interna (AISI) focuses on domestic intelligence within Italy. This was a prime target for the CIA—precisely what their "Trust, but verify" rule was designed for. Having a reliable source of internal information from the "Targets," own gathering Agency was, in the words of the leadership in The Company, "Priceless."

Biagio Caruso found his niche within the AISI, working as an analyst for the Italian government. Yet, unbeknownst to his employers, he was simultaneously serving the interests of the CIA. Caruso excelled in his dual role, adeptly gathering and transmitting the intelligence requested by the Agency. His skill and efficiency in managing this delicate "balance" made him an invaluable asset.

Meanwhile, Mike, relieved to "get out of that place," approached a clean-cut, good-looking man seated at a table in a beer garden. The setting was exactly as Christina had described, the perfect kind of place for Mike to relax. It was ideal for the discreet discussions that were about to take place. However, time was limited; Christina and Elena would be joining him soon. Mike had no intention of letting his Christina meet Caruso – it was something he decidedly wanted to "avoid." Perhaps it was out of loyalty to the Company, or maybe it was because Caruso was a very handsome man. More than likely, it was a little of both.

"Ahh, Mike, it's good to see you. It has been too long," Caruso stated, standing up to greet him with an extended hand. As he rose, his tall, 6'1″ stature and devilishly handsome looks became all too apparent. Dressed impeccably, his attire was the perfect blend of casual elegance and sophistication, suggesting a man who was comfortable being dressed to the nines in any setting. His captivating smile, bright and charming, resembled that of a model like Fabio, though Caruso's shorter, well-styled hair added to his distinct Northern Italian charm. His appearance, subtly reflecting his German, Scandinavian, and, of course, dominant Italian heritage, completed the picture of a man who was not just striking in looks but also had a presence that was both commanding and welcoming.

"Hello, Bigs; yes, it has. Thanks for helping with this," Mike replied, shaking his hand firmly.

"Of course. But I have to admit, I was a bit puzzled when Markus called. Everyone knows General Wu, but if he were here, we would likely have some insight. There's been nothing on the wire, at least nothing the Italian authorities are aware of."

"Yeah, it was unexpected for me too. But I have solid intel that he's in town and will attend the Gala tonight. I'm hoping to set up a 'meeting.'"

Biagio paused, weighing his words carefully. "Mike, I get your vendetta with the General, but not at the Gala. If the Duchessa finds out, we could have a serious problem."

The name "Duchessa," or Dutchess, held significant weight in this context. Biagio referred to Prime Minister Fiamma Silenziosa, formerly a well-known model who graced runways and magazine covers, now an influential political figure. She was expected at the Gala's opening ceremony and the main event showcasing Cavallaro's latest line.

"And Mike, I am not sure you two are on speaking terms, are you? I have only heard rumors, but if even half of what I heard is true... Dude..."

"Damn, I didn't know she'd be there. Okay, I need to rethink this," Mike mused, his thoughts drifting to Christina and her knack for uncovering his past romances. She always seemed to sense when he was keeping something hidden, especially an old flame. However, this was no ordinary fling; his time with the Duchess had turned his world upside down, leaving him with lingering anger. *Shit!*

"No, it's all good; I can handle her. I need you to get me a few things..." Mike began outlining his needs: information on the General's location, suitable "equipment" for when the time came, and additional security for Christina, specifically guards she hadn't encountered before, to prevent her from "giving them the slip" as she had become so skilled at doing.

"Next, let's get a couple of guys to shadow Elena too. I know she already has her own detail, but having locals on hand wouldn't hurt," Mike suggested.

Biagio hesitated, a note of caution in his voice. "Ahh, I do not want to step on your toes, but the Chief is my boss. Hell, she is your boss, too, brother.

If she finds out you are having her shadowed without her knowing... man, I just do not know. Things could become, 'real,' and quick."

"Don't worry about my wife; I can handle her. Just do as I ask. Oh, and one more thing. Make it Chinese weapons and ammo. When I make my move, the U.S. needs plausible deniability." Mike's request was clear and precise. He needed to operate discreetly, ensuring every detail was meticulously managed to avoid any direct ties to any U.S. involvement. But in reality, his primary concern was to keep Markus out of the line of fire.

"Va bene, you've got it, paisan. Just remember, I warned you," Biagio stated, his voice tinged with humor and caution. He let out a loud laugh, the sound echoing in the air, as he downed his second beer.

The Maestro:

Christina and Elena applauded the Maestro's masterpieces after most of the gowns had been showcased. Elena was still reeling from the revelation of their cost, while Christina was beaming with delight.

"If you ladies would please wait here, there is someone who wishes to speak with you," Ambrosia requested, gesturing for them to take their time exploring the store.

"Of course, no problem. I can't wait to see the rest of the shop anyway. Is it okay if we walk around?" Christina asked eagerly.

"Certo, please, feel free. You are our guests. I will be right back," Ambrosia responded before leaving them to browse.

Elena watched as Christina gleefully explored, her happiness evident in her smile and even in her humming. "You're having a good time, aren't you?" She asked, a smile tugging at her lips.

"Are you kidding? I'm having the time of my life! Elena, I love this place, these things... They're amazing," Christina exclaimed. Turning to her, she playfully added, "You know, it's your fault I have a taste for such nice things now. I was perfectly happy with off-the-rack clothes before I met you. But then, when I think about it, it's actually Mike's fault. It was his idea for you to look after me, so yeah, it's definitely his fault."

Elena brushed off Christina's comment, "I'm not sure what you mean. I was in town, and Mike asked if I could drive you around, that's all," she responded, addressing the half-question, half-remark.

However, Christina saw the comment as an opportunity to transition into a new conversation, one she had wanted to initiate but never found the right moment. Today, it felt like a suitable time.

"Elena, do you know what my best asset is?" she asked curiously.

"Your best asset? I think I'm looking at it right now," Elena replied with a playful smile.

Christina glanced over her shoulder, following Elena's gaze to her backside, then twisted around. "No, not that asset. I mean my true asset," she clarified with a smile of her own.

"Christina, you are one of the most beautiful women in the world; you have many assets. But what do you mean?"

"All my life, or at least as long as I can remember, people have always commented on my looks. 'Oh dear, you're so cute,' or 'That smile!' But they never really noticed anything beyond my face. Then, as I grew older and my body changed, the compliments shifted to, 'Wow, you're so beautiful.' Just like you pointed out," Christina continued, acknowledging Elena's earlier remark.

"Don't get me wrong, I love being called gorgeous and sexy, and I definitely love how I look. I'm sure you know that. But this..." motioning to her body "isn't my biggest asset. My real advantage is that, because of all this, people underestimate me. They think I'm just another pretty face—shallow, maybe even a bit dense, and totally unaware of what's happening around me. But Elena, I can assure you, that's far from the truth."

Elena looked surprised, concerned that her playful comment might have come across as an insult. "Hey, I didn't mean anything by it when I mentioned your... well, you know. I was just having fun," she said quickly, wanting to clear any misunderstanding. "I know you're intelligent, Christina, and I think everyone else recognizes that too."

Christina's tone was light but carried a hint of seriousness. "It's okay, Elena. I know you didn't mean anything by it. And I appreciate that you like me, too." She gave a wink and continued, "You see, being underestimated is not just an asset; it's like my superpower. It lets me get away with a lot, and more importantly, I get to know things without having to reveal what I know. Take, for instance, your job – the one you love so much that you 'just couldn't leave it for the family.' You claim to be the assistant to the Assistant Ambassador to France. But come on, Elena, you're not anyone's assistant. That's just laughable. No, I believe you're something much more important than that. I bet you have assistants of your own, and you're definitely not a diplomat." Her words were playful, yet they hinted at a deeper understanding of Elena's true role.

Elena was taken aback by Christina's insight. She had always known she was perceptive but hadn't anticipated this level of understanding. Her curiosity was piqued, leading her to probe further. "So, what are you implying, Christina? What do you think I do?"

Christina leaned in slightly, her voice laced with certainty. "First off, I think you and Mike work together. I'm not entirely sure what it is you both do, but it definitely isn't tech-related. I mean, Mike is the biggest technophobe I know. He gets locked out of his iPhone almost every week and always needs my help to fix it. And don't even get me started on computers; the guy can barely open a file. He's no IT Tech. That's for sure."

She paused for a moment before continuing. "But he does have other skills, skills I've seen firsthand. Things he knows how to do, things I've witnessed. I don't like thinking about it, but Mike's job is... well, it's darker than just an IT Tech. And I have a feeling yours is similar." Her tone was serious now, indicating she had put quite some thought into this theory.

Elena quickly reminded her, "You know he was a Navy SEAL, right? Those skills you're talking about, he learned them there."

"Yeah, no. I'm sure that's part of it. But it's not the whole story," Christina replied. She chose her words carefully before continuing. "Elena, when we started this trip, Mike was so upbeat. I even heard him whistle, and I swear, he skipped out of the train car. But then, something shifted in him. It wasn't a drastic change, but he seemed distant, preoccupied. Like something, or someone, was weighing on his mind. Then you showed up. Don't get me wrong, I'm thrilled you're here. But why? You said you couldn't meet us at your place in Paris, yet here you are. In Milan?"

Christina's tone conveyed a mix of curiosity and understanding. "And then there are the two guys who've been tailing us. They're with you, aren't they? I doubt you'd let Mike assign two bodyguards to shadow you like he does with me. So, who are they? Don't worry; I'm not expecting you to spill. Oh, and then there's the President of the United States who stops by for golf on the weekends? He brings his girlfriend and stays at the ranch. What IT Tech hangs out with the President? Come on, sheesh,"

Elena responded, her voice laced with a blend of admiration and serious-ness, "Little miss, you are definitely not stupid. I realized that the first day we met. Yes, Mike and I work together, and those men are indeed with me. However, I can't tell you more than that. And Christina, believe me when I say this: Don't tell Mike what you suspect. I'm pretty sure he already has an inkling of your suspicions. But you mean the world to him. If he finds out what you think you know, it will crush him."

"I know. For all his strengths, the guy really is a giant pussy when it comes to me. That's why I'm telling you, not him. Whatever you two are here to do, I want to help."

Elena was visibly surprised, the gravity of Christina's offer and her own inability to involve her weighing heavily. She knew allowing Christina even the slightest insight into their plans could be risky. Yet, seeing the genuine willingness in her eyes, she felt compelled to respond.

"Christina, honestly, we're not here on any special job," she began, but she could see the disappointment on Christina's face, knowing that once again she was being lied to. "Alright, we are here on business. But you can't help with that. Or wait, maybe there is a way you can..." Elena trailed off, her mind racing to find a safe yet meaningful way for Christina to contribute without compromising their Mission or, more frankly, her and Mike's relationship.

The two women continued their conversation until a group of four – two men and two women – approached them. The group's leader, a man clearly from the fashion world, was a picture of sartorial elegance. He sported a shirt left casually unbuttoned at the top, revealing a full chest of hair. His walk was purposeful, the others seemingly hustling to keep pace.

Right behind him, one woman, exceptionally tall with long black hair, multitasked between her tablet and a headset. The other woman, shorter with striking flame-red dyed hair, carried a laptop and conversed with the leading man as she walked. The last member of the group was a man with a hippie-like appearance, featuring long, wavy brown hair and a short beard. An expensive, almost antique-looking camera hung around his neck.

Their approach was brisk and purposeful, causing Elena to pause and subtly reach behind her back, murmuring something nearly inaudible.

Christina, recognizing the defensive gesture and having seen Mike make similar moves, quickly reached out to Elena's arm to reassure her that these newcomers posed no threat.

Meanwhile, Elena was wearing an earpiece, a direct line to the men stationed outside. Unbeknownst to Christina, at the Chief's command, they were poised to burst through the showroom's locked door, ready for action at a moment's notice.

"Ah-ha, you must be the famous Christina McHaskell I've heard so much about," the leading man said as he reached out, gently taking her hands and holding her arms out to their sides, appraising her with an expert eye. He then turned to Elena, "And you. You are as beautiful as described, and that figure. Yes, you are quite exquisite, aren't you?"

Elena, slightly stunned, whispered something while covering her mouth, her eyes flicking back to Christina. Meanwhile, the man had started to spin Christina around, examining her with the keen interest of an artist assessing a perfect canvas.

"Yes, this body, I simply must have it," he said, his tone a mixture of professional admiration and artistic excitement.

"Excuse me? Have her? I don't think so, buddy," Elena interjected, moving to intervene against the man's forwardness. But Christina quickly stepped in.

"It's okay, Elena, this is..."

"Oh my, so sorry for my absentmindedness. I presumed everyone knew of me. Allow me to introduce myself," the man interrupted with a flourish. "I am Lorenzo Cavallaro, at your service." His tone was a blend of flamboyance and charm, typical of someone accustomed to the grandeur and drama of the fashion world.

"It's such an honor to meet you, Mr. Cavallaro. I had no idea you would be here today. Gosh...." Christina acted as if she were in the presence of royalty. Something Elena wasn't too fond of, and if Mike were here, things would have turned for the worse.

Cavallaro moved to Elena, taking in her bust with both hands. He pushed them together and then lifted them up. "Hmm, I do not believe I had the proper measurements for these, but no worries, I will ensure your gown is adjusted for this evening," he remarked, scrutinizing Elena's figure with a professional eye. With a snap of his fingers, the woman wearing the headset began to speak, efficiently relaying the Maestro's instructions to someone on the other end.

Elena, shocked by Cavallaro's forwardness, managed to quip with a hint of sarcasm, "Gettin mighty friendly, aren't we?"

Christina, unfazed and amused, chuckled as Cavallaro turned his attention back to her. "Christina McHaskell... This simply will not do. From now on, you will be known as just Christina. Like Cher, Madonna, and Elle. There is no room for McHaskell in that echelon. And this dress... it is not right for you. I need to see the real you. Please, disrobe," Cavallaro declared, gesturing for her to undress in his straightforward, no-nonsense fashion typical of someone used to working in the high-paced world of fashion design.

Christina, not accustomed to the direct and often intrusive world of high fashion, seemed motionless at the request. Elena, ever protective and assertive, quickly stepped in. "Yeah, I don't think so, Lorenzo; she stays dressed," she firmly stated.

Cavallaro looked genuinely confused at this response. He glanced at his entourage, who shared his puzzled expression. "I am sorry, I do not understand. Bailey assured me that you would be cooperative. Christina, I have poured my heart into crafting your outfits for the show. I need to ensure they fit perfectly. My dear, this performance is paramount for my legacy, and it is poised to be a significant launch for your career," he explained.

"But Mr. Cavallaro, I'm confident the dress will be just fine. Besides, I'm just one face in the crowd. I doubt I'll draw much attention," Christina responded.

Cavallaro's expression shifted to one of even greater confusion. "Signora, I believe there has been a significant misunderstanding. You see, Christina, you are not just a part of the show; you... are the centerpiece of tomorrow night's event. You are my Cleopatra, my Queen of the Nile. Has our Bailey not explained this all to you?"

The Gala:

"Ladies, please, we're going to be late," Mike called out from the living room. In truth, he wasn't particularly eager for them to leave for the event. The thought of every man (and quite a few women) at the Gala admiring his wives wasn't exactly appealing. However, tonight was important to Christina, and there was also the slim chance that General Wu might make an appearance, which could work in his favor.

Mike had not disclosed to his wives that the Duchessa might be in attendance, nor had he revealed his past connection with her. He secretly hoped for some unforeseen political emergency requiring her presence elsewhere. But considering his luck, he thought, *she'll probably end up sitting right next to me.*

Elena emerged first, stepping out of her room in a dress that instantly captured his attention. The gown was a stunning shade of dark blue, elegantly designed to accentuate her figure in all the right places, though Mike thought it seemed a bit on the *thin* side. He couldn't help but wonder about the dress's "structural integrity," "Wow, Elena, you look amazing! Just wow, I'm speechless," he exclaimed.

"Thank you, Mike," Elena replied, her voice tinged with appreciation and discomfort. "Really, I feel kind of awkward in this..., if you can even call it a dress. It's more like... I don't know, lingerie?" She threw her hands up, a gesture of slight frustration. "What has Christina gotten me into?" Her half-joking, half-serious question reflected her uncertainty about the "daring" fashion choice.

"Nonsense, you look amazing, really. I'm just curious about how... you know," Mike asked, his voice trailing off as he gestured vaguely towards her bust.

"Tape, Mike. Lots and lots of tape," Elena replied with a hint of exasperation. "Do they look okay? I feel so squeezed in." She walked over to a full-length mirror mounted on the back wall, fussing with the dress in an attempt to adjust it. But it was clearly designed to make a "statement," leaving little room for adjustment.

Mike's thoughts then drifted to his Christina. Knowing her "style," which tended to be even more on the "fearless" side, he couldn't help but imagine what her outfit would look like. A sense of unease settled over him as he contemplated the evening ahead.

Elena caught the look on his face and turned around to address him. "Mike, she's a grown woman, and it's her body, so let her be. I haven't seen her dress yet, and I'm sure your worries are well-founded. But remember, it's fashion week, and we're in Europe. Things here aren't like they are back home. Just let her be herself."

Mike could only grunt in response to Elena's comment, his attention shifting as the door to the other bedroom opened. Christina stepped out, and he was instantly struck by her appearance. She was breathtaking, though Mike felt a pang of discomfort at the thought of others seeing her like this.

Christina's dress was a stunning, bright red, sideless halter gown. It was unafraid in design, with a slight fabric that wrapped around her neck, crossing just over her chest to provide minimal coverage. The gown then plunged into a low v that barely covered her lower waist, extending to her feet. A delicate gold chain encircled her waist, holding another swath of fabric covering her back, offering just a glimpse of her backside. The material seemed almost magical, clinging to her figure and leaving little to the imagination. Her physique, a statement of her dedication to fitness and training with Parker, was on full display, sculpted, and defined.

Mike took in the sight before him, a mix of pride and apprehension etched on his face. He was clearly proud of the fruits of her hard work, yet he felt uneasy about the attention she was bound to attract. "My God! Babe!" he finally managed to say, his voice a blend of awe and surprise. He stood momentarily speechless, absorbing the stunning sight of his Christina.

"Do you like it?" she asked, her voice tinged with a hint of nervous excitement as she slowly spun around to showcase the full effect of her dress.

"Yes, I do! You look great, really great, Babe," he replied, his initial shock giving way to an admiring approval.

Elena, equally captivated by Christina's look, added her own praise. "Wow, Christina, you look so good. Just awesome, good job, girl."

Christina's smile broadened at their reactions. "Thank you both," she responded, a sense of relief in her voice. "Mike, I was worried you might not want me to wear this, but I really like it."

In truth, if Mike had his way, Christina wouldn't be wearing that dress—or anything remotely resembling it. But the words of both Elena and Claire resonated in his mind. Claire had specifically advised him to relax, to let Christina embrace her desires, and to just go with it—to have fun if he could.

He responded to Christina, "Of course, Honey, you're your own person. I wouldn't tell you what to wear. Even if I can see your..."

Before he could finish his sentence, Elena interjected, steering the conversation away from potentially awkward territory. "Okay, let's get going, shall we?"

Arriving at the Gala was a spectacle in itself. The event was held at the Terrazza del Duomo, a rooftop venue renowned for its breathtaking views of the Duomo di Milano. This cathedral, the epitome of Milanese splendor, was one of the largest Gothic cathedrals in the world and a landmark of Italy.

Fashion Week in Milan was a quintessential gathering of the crème de la crème in the fashion world. It attracted a diverse and illustrious crowd—from renowned designers to celebrities, politicians, and billionaires. Everyone who's anyone in the fashion industry and beyond would be in attendance, making it a preeminent event of style, glamour, and influence.

The high-profile nature of the Gala also made it a relatively safe place for Christina. By now, the General was likely aware of Mike's presence in the city. Given the deep animosity between him and the General, coupled with the fact that the Chinese often didn't adhere to the "family is off-limits" rule, Mike had been on edge since learning of the man's presence in Milan. Conversely, the same high-profile nature of the Gala that protected Christina also shielded the General... from Mike. With attendees including a wide array of influential figures, the event was not a place where he could "confront" the man as he might have wished.

However, he would remain alert, ready to seize any opportunity that might arise to "deal" with his "Target" should the right moment present itself. But as often happens, life had other plans for Mike McHaskell.

As their limousine pulled up to the venue, it was immediately besieged by a barrage of flashing lights and a crowd of bodies, all clamoring to capture the first photograph of the vehicle's occupants. The trio in the back of the limousine were surprised by the frenzy. None of them were celebrities, and even though they came from wealth, that wasn't public knowledge—at least not here.

One of Elena's security detail was the first to step out. After quickly assessing the crowd and conferring with his colleagues already at the event for security overwatch, he moved towards the rear passenger door. Two men on a red carpet gestured for him to open it. The first to emerge was Christina. As soon as she stepped out, she was instantly engulfed by a barrage of flashing bulbs that illuminated her every move. Unaccustomed to such attention, her eyes were momentarily blinded, causing her to look back at Mike, who was now exiting the vehicle. Before she could reach for his hand, one of the men on the carpet extended his own towards her.

"Christina! Please, this way. I am going to introduce you to the world," Lorenzo Cavallaro called out, beckoning her forward with enthusiasm and urgency.

Seeing his Christina being pulled away by someone he didn't know amidst all the commotion, Mike was understandably upset. He quickly jumped to her aid, unaware she wasn't in any danger. "Get your hands off her," he yelled, pushing Cavallaro to the ground and pulling Christina away from his grasp. He then positioned himself between what he perceived as a threat to his mate.

Surrounded by paparazzi, all eager to capture the next million-dollar front-page image, a blood-filled frenzy commenced, like hungry sharks feasting on the weeping carcass of an injured seal.

Shocked by the swift action and now standing behind him, Christina yelled, "Mike, no! He's the Maestro; it's okay!"

Stunned but poised as usual, Cavallaro rose to his feet and composed himself. He turned to the onslaught of clicking shutters and jokingly expressed, "Americans, always in such a hurry." Approaching Mike, he continued, "You must be the uomo our Bailey talks so much about. It is so nice to meet you, Signore McHaskell; I am Lorenzo Cavallaro, at your service."

Christina quickly stepped toward Cavallaro, brushing off his "fabulous" jacket and straightening the rest of his ensemble. "I am so sorry, Mr. Cavallaro. My husband can be a bit impulsive sometimes. He didn't mean anything by it."

Cavallaro, not stunned, took her hands, smiled, and responded, "No need, my dear. And please, call me Lorenzo. We are business partners now." He then turned back to Mike. "I am sorry for the confusion, Mr. McHaskell. I had thought Signora Bailey had explained everything. No matter, I shall..."

Before he could finish, Elena arrived, clearly unhappy with her husband. "Thanks for the help out there, Mike. I see where I rank."

The look on Mike's face, with its etched stone-coldness, black eyes, and unflinching stare that would have intimidated most, if not anyone, had little to no effect on Cavallaro. In fact, it seemed as if he didn't even notice. It wasn't until Elena grabbed Mike's arm to ensure he heard her that his expression softened, although not by much.

"Mike? Hellooooo! MIKE!" she yelled.

"Oh yeah, I'm sorry, Elena, I was just surprised," Mike replied. Turning to Christina, he asked, "Babe, why didn't you tell me you too knew each other."

Now holding Cavallaro's arm, Christina responded softly, "I'm sorry, Honey. I was going to explain, but time got away from me."

Cavallaro suggested, "Ladies, perhaps we should take this conversation out of the public eye. Christina, will you please accompany me? I have some very important people you should meet."

Without waiting for Mike's acknowledgment, Cavallaro and Christina were on the move. Elena took Mike's arm and gently whispered, "It's okay, my husband. I forgive you. You jerk!"

Mike, unfazed, stared at Christina, now posing for photographs next to one of the world's most renowned fashion designers. The man pointed at her gown, smiling and joking with the paparazzi. *What the Fuc... is going on?* He asked himself.

Inside the venue, the grandeur of the Terrazza del Duomo on the opening night of Milan's Fashion Week unfolded in a spectacle of glamour. The Grand Hall, illuminated by an array of crystal chandeliers, cast a radiant glow over the elegantly dressed guests. Luxurious drapes in rich fabrics trimmed the walls, complementing the marble floors that gleamed underfoot, reflecting the soft light.

At the center of the room, a magnificent staircase served as a focal point, with guests occasionally pausing for impromptu photo sessions. The air was filled with the light, harmonious notes of classical music played by a live orchestra positioned on a raised dais, their melodies weaving through the conversations and laughter.

Waiters and waitresses, embodying sophistication in their black-tie attire, glided through the crowd with silver trays laden with gourmet hors d'oeuvres and champagne. The aroma of the exquisite food mingled with the subtle scents of expensive perfumes. At the bar, skilled mixologists crafted cocktails, and the pop of champagne corks punctuated the hum of conversation as flutes of the sparkling beverage were passed around.

Everywhere, the elite of the fashion world mingled. Designers, models, celebrities, and influencers formed a vibrant tapestry of the crème de la crème. Their conversations, a mix of various languages, buzzed with excitement and anticipation for the week's events.

Mike, amidst this opulence, couldn't help but perceive the air of pretension among the glitterati. Their laughter seemed to ring a bit too loud, their gestures a bit too grandiose, embodying what he saw as the most pretentious aspects of high society. Yet, Mike knew Christina would be in awe of the undeniable allure of the event, the sheer spectacle of it all. For her, he was willing to endure anything—even this.

He and Elena found themselves standing at the bar, where Mike wanted a stiff scotch, perhaps two or maybe four. Elena seemed eager to help him achieve this goal. In her mind, a lubricated Mike was a controllable Mike.

"Elena, what the hell is going on? Why is Christina hobnobbing with that guy? And what was that comment about Bailey?" Mike asked, visibly confused and frustrated.

Elena sighed before responding. "I was hoping Christina would have told you. But I had a sneaking suspicion she might not." She picked up one of the cocktail napkins sitting on top of the bar and then continued. "You throw a nice party, Mike, really nice."

"What are you talking about? I throw a nice party? I hate being here. I'm only here for her... Oh, and you, of course."

"Haha!" Elena laughed. "Not for me, you made that painfully obvious." She handed him the napkin. "You see, this is your party and your guests, Mr. McHaskell."

Mike's eyes furrowed as he unfolded the napkin, which was black with an unmistakable logo in the center: 'McHaskell Enterprises' in silver.

"What the... Elena, why is OUR name on this napkin?" He quickly looked around, suddenly taking in the sight of his name plastered about the event.

"I think you should ask your wife, Mike. Bailey set this up, not me. Also, you might want to ask her why she 'pimped out' Christina. Just saying."

"She what? What do you mean 'pimped out' Christina? To who?" he quickly grabbed his phone and started dialing frantically. Elena grabbed his hand.

"No, Mike, I was joking. Leave Bailey alone. Everything will be fine. Let me explain." Elena went on to describe the connection she knew of between Lorenzo and Bailey. She revealed how their family owned fifty percent of Cavallaro's empire and that Christina was now the feature model for his new line. She left out Christina's exact role, thinking it better to disclose that later after the scotch had taken effect.

"But Christina isn't a model. Yeah, she's gorgeous; I mean, just look at her. But aren't models," he motioned to a woman walking by the couple, "like her? Tall, no boobs, sickly looking?"

Elena shook her head as the woman took offense to Mike's comments. She apologized for her husband's unkind words, then turned back to him. "Mike, look at her. This whole place is enamored with her. Of course, she'll make a great showcase for the Maestro's endeavors. Bailey must've seen this. Have you ever known her to lose money? No, of course not. Bailey found Christina to be an asset, and I don't blame her; she is an asset."

Mike was visibly agitated. "She is my wife, and not for sale. Goddamn it," he muttered as he reached for his phone again. This time, Elena didn't stop him. She knew exactly whom he was calling, and it wasn't Bailey.

"Claire... What the hell is going on? Did you know..." Mike's voice trailed off as he began his conversation.

Elena observed why Claire was so integral to The Agency. Her words, tone, and everything about her manner of speaking came together perfectly, soothing the hot-blooded assassin in just a few seconds. In what Elena estimated was no more than two minutes, Claire had not only refocused Mike's mind but also brought him peace, allowing him to return to the real reason for his presence there—General Wu. Of course, Claire likely didn't know that she was facilitating this.

"Do you feel better now?" Claire inquired soothingly.

"Yes, Honey, thank you. I just... I mean, you know it's Christina. She's mine, not something to be exploited. I don't like this, that's all," Mike replied, his voice carrying a mix of protectiveness and frustration.

"Of course she is, Mike, and she will always be. You know that. Don't worry, Christina can make up her own mind. And besides, I bet she's loving every minute of it, isn't she?"

Mike's gaze had not left Christina since they arrived. Observing her now, she indeed seemed to be having the time of her life. "Yes, Honey, you are right. Okay, we can let this play out. Thank you again. Kiss my children for me. I love you."

"I know you do. Now go have fun. I'll talk to you later," Claire concluded before hanging up.

"Well, all fixed?" Elena asked as Mike put his phone back in his pocket.

He only grunted in response, quickly downing his second scotch. Looking at the bartender, he ordered, "One more, this time the good stuff, and make it a four-finger. It's on my dime anyway, right?" he motioned with his hands. Typically, a four-finger pour would mean the height of four fingers held sideways. But Mike wanted four fingers straight up, his hand gesture emphasizing the difference. The bartender laughed, understanding the request, and nodded in agreement.

As the fourth scotch began to take effect, Mike's demeanor visibly calmed. He remained fixated on Christina's every move, yet he allowed her to continue mingling freely. Their constant eye contact persisted while she walked around, engaging with everyone Cavallaro introduced her to. The look of disgust that had been prominent on Mike's face earlier began to fade, becoming less intense with each passing moment.

"Okay, if you'll be fine for a minute, I need to use the ladies' room. Promise me you won't start any trouble and stay right here," Elena requested.

"Yes, Honey, I'm fine," he replied.

Elena smiled at him and walked off. Mike watched her leave, a mixture of reluctance and admiration in his gaze. He couldn't help but think,

That Cavallaro Guy really is a maestro with fabric. For the first time that evening, a smile crossed his face.

"Ahh, Agent Jones, quite the unexpected pleasure to see you here this evening," a voice, all too familiar and unsettling, rang out. Its menacing coldness struck at the very core of Mike's soul.

Mike's eyes narrowed as he responded, not turning his head to meet the voice's owner, "Hello, General. I hoped we might meet tonight." His smile turned more sinister and devious, hinting at an alternative plan rapidly forming in his mind.

The General, flanked by his two guards, now stood beside Mike, who leaned casually against the bar. Turning to face them, Mike's expression revealed his malicious intent towards the General.

"Was that Chief Alvarez? I have not had the chance to see her since the summit in Beijing last winter. It will be truly delightful for us to... 'reunite.'" the General remarked, his words laced with a sinister grin of his own.

Mike chuckled at the thought; *yeah, right,* he mused to himself, then replied, "Yes. She'll be right back," while his eyes subtly addressed the guards. In his estimation, each appeared to be about five and a half feet tall, dressed in black suits with sunglasses. Both men had their hands positioned under their jackets, likely cradling their QSZ-92 9mm pistols. Mike surmised that each guard would carry a minimum of 30 rounds of ammunition, possibly some type of tactical knife, and would be meticulously trained in martial arts. *No problem,* he concluded inwardly, confident in his own skills.

"You know, General, I've been looking forward to this meeting, especially since our last encounter was cut short by you running away and all," he stated with a hint of taunting.

The General, his right hand gliding over his cheek to the eye patch covering his eye, responded with a cool, calculated tone. "Yes, indeed, during that occasion, you held the upper hand, Mr. Jones – or should I address you as Mr. McHaskell. As you can observe, the scales have tipped decidedly in my favor this evening. And yes, you are correct; this reunion has been long overdue. However, I am inclined to think the outcome will not be as beneficial for you as our previous meeting." His voice was a blend of confidence and underlying threat.

"Good then. Shall we?" Mike gestured towards the back of the hall, in the direction of the kitchen.

"Indeed, we shall," the General replied, nodding in agreement.

"Shall what? Gentlemen." Elena's voice cut through the tension as she approached.

Shit, I almost had him... Mike thought to himself. Aloud, he replied, "Nothing, Elena. The General and I were just reminiscing about old times."

"Ahhh, Chief Alvarez, it is a pleasure to see you. I was just recounting our previous encounter in Beijing with Agent Jones. It is wonderful to reconnect, is it not? And that dress, my dear, is absolutely stunning." the General answered, his words dripping with his usual politeness and a hint of ulterior motive.

"Thank you, General. Would you care to escort me to meet with the Prime Minister? I believe she has just arrived," Elena asked, her smile masking the strategic play she was making.

The General offered his arm to the stunning Latin beauty. "Of course, let us proceed."

As the two walked away, the General made a quick but determined hand gesture to his guards. Each acknowledged the signal, exchanged a brief look, and then turned their attention to Mike, their intent clear in their focused gaze.

Mike, catching the General's gesture and now facing the unwavering stare of the guards, responded with a calm yet defiant tone, "So I guess it's our turn to dance. That's fine by me, boys. Lead on."

A Welcomed Battle:

The three men entered the kitchen, their entrance choreographed like a tense procession. One guard led the way, with Mike following closely behind and the other guard taking up the rear. As they pushed through the swinging double doors, they were instantly confronted with the bustling chaos of a commercial kitchen in full swing.

The air was thick with the aromas of gourmet dishes being prepared, a sensory overload contrasting sharply with the tension between the men. Chefs in crisp white uniforms moved deftly between stoves and countertops, their focused expressions a stark contrast to the guards' stern faces. Waiters and waitresses, along with busboys, darted in and out, carrying trays of food or clearing utensils, oblivious to the undercurrent of hostility that had just entered their domain.

The clatter of pots and pans, the sizzle of food frying on the griddle, and the occasional shouted orders from the Head Chef added to the cacophony. The bright fluorescent lights illuminated every corner of the kitchen, casting stark shadows and giving the stainless steel surfaces an almost sterile gleam.

Mike knew he couldn't allow himself to be led out of the venue. He was certain the General had a surprise waiting for him outside, likely far more perilous than anything inside this kitchen. He needed to dispatch these men before they reached the outer doors, which he assumed led to the alley out back. As they moved through the space, Mike's eyes quickly scanned the environment, formulating a plan.

In a kitchen, numerous items can be improvised for self-defense. Beyond the obvious choices like knives, pots, pans, and rolling pins, many seemingly benign items can become effective defensive weaponry in the face of an attacker.

Take salt and pepper, for instance. Salt, when thrown into the eyes of an assailant, can act as a potent disabling agent. It rapidly dehydrates the eyes, causing temporary blindness and disorientation, thus allowing the victim a critical window for a safe exit. This simple kitchen staple, often overlooked, can be a quick and effective tool in thwarting an attack.

Pepper, on the other hand, can be used to disrupt an attacker's breathing. A quick blast directed at the nose and mouth can induce coughing and choking, impairing the assailant's ability to pursue or attack further. This can provide the victim with a vital opportunity to escape and seek help.

In a life-or-death situation, where every second counts, such everyday items can be ingeniously repurposed for self-preservation.

Of course, escape was not Mike's objective. He was on a Mission, and eliminating two of the General's men was a necessary item on his to-do list. His eyes, sharp and calculating, surveyed the area not for an exit but for tools to aid in his objective. The bustling environment, with its array of utensils and culinary implements, provided a diverse arsenal for someone with Mike's skills and purpose.

The lead guard, oblivious to Mike's intentions, continued to advance, but Mike was primed for action. With a swift and fluid motion, he seized a boiling pot of water from a nearby stove using a towel, swinging it with lethal precision. The pot struck the lead guard on the side of the head, sending him reeling from the unexpected blow and scalding water.

The second guard reacted almost instantly, reaching under his jacket for his weapon. But Mike was quicker. He lunged backward, propelling the guard against a stainless-steel prep table. The collision of bodies against the metal echoed through the kitchen, briefly overpowering the ambient sounds. Mike's hand shot out, targeting precise pressure points on the man's neck and clavicle, rendering him incapacitated in seconds.

Turning back to the first guard, who was now struggling to regain his composure and prepare for a counterattack, Mike didn't hesitate. He delivered a powerful forward kick with his right leg, striking the man's chest. The force sent the guard flying backward, crashing into a rack of hanging pasta.

The sounds of their struggle filled the air, a chaotic symphony amidst the kitchen's rhythm. To Mike's surprise, the skirmish seemed to go unnoticed by the busy staff, absorbed in their culinary tasks. Quickly, he refocused on the confrontation, his senses heightened, ready to react to any further threats. This was not just a fight; it was a calculated objective, each move a critical part of his strategy.

Steel in his eyes and a hint of a smirk on his lips, Mike squared himself up, ready for the next move. This smile wasn't one of malice but rather a reflection of his enjoyment of the challenge. Truth be told, he was indeed enjoying himself. The rigorous training sessions with Parker had been invaluable, sharpening his skills and reflexes. She was his equal in every physical aspect, pushing him to his limits and unknowingly preparing him for moments like these.

Now, here he was, in the midst of a heated confrontation, facing two adversaries who were on the receiving end of his finely honed abilities. Each move he made was a testament to his preparedness and skill, sharpened through relentless practice and discipline. This was more than a mere physical confrontation for Mike; it validated his training, strength, and strategy. He was fully immersed in the moment, his body and mind in perfect sync, reveling in the intensity of the battle.

Suddenly, a sharp pain accompanied by the unmistakable sound of ribs shattering broke through the intensity of the fight. Mike clutched his side just after the first guard had swung a stainless steel rod, landing a heavy blow to Mike's right side. After crashing through the rack of hanging pasta, the guard had found his improvised weapons: two metal rods, originally part of the rack used to cook macaroni in a specially designed boiler.

Mike turned to face the man, his expression changing. The playful demeanor he had previously exhibited was gone, replaced by a deadly resolve. It was clear that the moment for toying with his opponents had passed, and now it was time to end this confrontation decisively.

His movements became more calculated and lethal, driven by a mix of pain and determination. Mike's training and instinct took over, each move precise and aimed to neutralize the threat efficiently. The kitchen, once a place of culinary creation, had turned into an arena where every object could be a weapon, and every action could be the difference between victory and dire consequences. Mike, despite his injury, was ready to bring this unexpected battle to a swift and conclusive end.

Seizing the opportunity, he lunged at the guard, his movements, driven this time, by raw anger. He grabbed the man firmly, using his momentum to pull him toward the specialized boiler. With a swift motion, he slammed the guard's head against the stainless steel frame, then, in one fluid movement, plunged him headfirst into the boiling water. Mike held him there, his grip unyielding, just long enough to ensure the guard was forever incapacitated. Finally, he released, letting the man slump to the ground with a heavy thud. In a grim parallel, just as countless crustaceans had met their fate in boiling water over the eons, the guard, too, found his end in a similar fashion.

Then, turning to face the remaining guard, Mike took up the metal rods the first guard had used – one in each hand. He launched into a barrage of attacks, each strike precise and ruthless. He targeted the head, neck, and torso, his every move a demonstration of his lethal intent. The final blow, a decisive strike to the top of the man's head, ended the confrontation instantly.

The kitchen, now silent except for the faint sizzle of the boiling water, bore witness to the fierce and swift resolution of the battle. Mike stood, catching his breath, the aftermath of his actions evident in the stillness that followed.

The kitchen staff, still seemingly unfazed by the violence that had just unfolded, continued about their business as if nothing had happened. The only acknowledgment came from the Head Chef, who took notice of the scene. Instead of reacting with alarm, he simply nodded at Mike, his gesture implying a silent commendation—"Well done." This unexpected approval took Mike by surprise, but he had little time to ponder it; he had two now lifeless bodies to deal with.

With caution, He slowly opened the back door of the venue, half-expecting to confront the next phase of the General's plan. He peered out, ready for whatever lay in wait, but to his surprise, the alley was clear. The anticipated ambush or trap from the General was nowhere to be seen. This unexpected twist left him momentarily puzzled but also provided a brief respite. The quiet, deserted alley offered a stark contrast to the chaos and intensity of the kitchen battleground he had just left behind.

Mike dragged the bodies outside and deposited them into a nearby dumpster. He quickly took a photo of the scene and sent it off with a text, then set about straightening his appearance. After a few moments of tidying up, he prepared to re-enter the kitchen. Before opening the door, he braced himself, thinking, *Either there's going to be a throng of security guards, or the police. Be ready, Mike.*

However, just as when he had ventured into the alleyway, there was nothing. The entire sequence of events inside the kitchen had apparently been inconsequential, and the mess had already been cleaned up. "Well, isn't this the shit," he muttered to himself, surprise and relief in his voice. "Alright, let's get back to it."

As he re-entered the venue, Mike could feel the atmosphere of the Gala seeping back into his consciousness, a stark contrast to the fierce encounter he had just left behind. The shift from the adrenaline-fueled intensity of combat to the more serene and elegant setting of the event was jarring. With each step, the pain from his broken ribs became more pronounced, the adrenaline that had masked the discomfort during the fight now fading away.

Jeeeezzzus, he thought to himself, a mix of pain and realization washing over him. The physical toll of the confrontation was making itself known, each breath and movement reminding him of the encounter's brutality. Despite this, he maintained his composure, not wanting to draw attention or concern from the unsuspecting Gala attendees and, of course, his Christina.

As he navigated through the venue, his focus was now on finding Elena and Christina, the loves of his life, to reconnect with the normalcy and affection they represented. Amid the glamour and sophistication of the event, he sought the comfort and grounding their presence would provide, a necessary solace after the night's unexpected but very welcomed turn of events.

"That's affirmative, Ma'am, Mission accomplished... Yes, Mike 'executed' with distinction. He's one tough son of a bitch... Negative on any issues with the General's men. My team successfully neutralized the 'surprise' in the alley prior to commencement."

Agent Joe Harvey was on comms, briefing his superior on the operation's outcome. Stationed above the skirmish in the building across the alley, he reported, "Affirmative, Ma'am, the area will be sanitized before exfil... Appreciate that... will comply."

The Duchessa:

"What the hell happened to you?" Elena's voice was filled with concern. She was the first to notice Mike upon his return to the Gala. Her eyes quickly scanned him, picking up on the subtle changes in his demeanor and appearance that indicated something was amiss.

The General had been called away while they were engaging in conversation with the Prime Minister. Elena was unaware that the General's abrupt departure was likely connected to a conflict involving Mike and his guards.

Mike, trying to maintain his calm despite the pain from his injuries sustained during the recent altercation, quickly thought of a plausible explanation. He knew he had to tread carefully, not wanting to alarm Elena or reveal the true extent of what had transpired.

"Yeah, it's nothing. Just had a little mishap in the crowd," he said, trying to downplay the situation. His voice was steady, but those who knew him well could probably detect the faintest hint of strain. He adjusted his stance slightly in an attempt to ease the discomfort from his ribs while keeping his expression as neutral as possible.

Elena, however, seemed skeptical, her eyes still studying him with worry and suspicion. She clearly sensed there was more to the story than he was letting on.

"Mike, please, that line might work on the others but not on me, and you know it. Really, what happened?" She pressed, her tone indicating that she wouldn't accept a vague answer.

Mike sighed, realizing that Elena's perceptiveness meant he couldn't just brush off her concerns. "I guess the General had a plan for me. Sadly for him, it didn't go as he wished. But I'm okay, really. Now, where's Christina?" he deflected, trying to shift the focus.

Before Elena could respond, a familiar voice came from behind them. "Hey, there you are! Gosh, I've been looking all over for you. Madame Prime Minister, this is my husband, Mike." It was his Christina, her voice filled with excitement and warmth as she introduced her Mike.

Mike turned around to see her approaching with the Prime Minister. The pain from his ribs and the tension from the earlier altercation were momentarily pushed to the back of his mind as he prepared to greet the Duchess, mustering a smile and demeanor befitting the occasion. This, though seemingly fitting for the moment, was more of a vague cover, a skill not just for masking the evening's events but a relic from a previous lifetime. One that included him and the Duchess.

Years earlier, as one of the youngest SEAL Team Leaders to date, Mike had distinguished himself not only through his remarkable achievements and accolades but also as a legacy member, leading the same team his father had done just a few years earlier. His duties were diverse and often high-profile.

As part of a broader initiative to enhance the military's public image and strengthen international relations, then President Nelson issued a directive that swept Mike into what he considered the realm of "politics." He was ordered to attend the "Unity for Peace" Charity Ball in Rome, Italy, an event designed to promote peace and support war-torn regions. The Gala was a magnet for celebrities, philanthropists, and influential figures from all corners of the globe.

The occasion also marked the entrance of the "Duchessa," the renowned Fiamma Silenziosa, into Mike's life. Still radiating the youth and glamour of a fashion model, Fiamma was a mesmerizing presence, capturing the attention of everyone, including Mike.

The young Master Chief, donning his finest military dress uniform, was equally striking. Standing tall at 6'5" with a formidable physique, his appearance was compelling. His smile, which hovered between a smirk and a grin, only added to his allure. He caught the Duchess's eye, drawing her in like a moth to a flame.

However, Fiamma Silenziosa was not one to be easily swayed. A woman who knew what she wanted and how to get it, she held her own, undaunted by the imposing figure before her. Despite his captivating presence, she remained a formation of power and determination, not easily influenced by even the most striking of individuals.

What started as a single night at the Gala quickly blossomed into a weekend, then unfurled into an entire week. It didn't take long for Mike to realize his feelings. He had fallen in love. The age gap between them, with Mike in his late twenties and Fiamma admitting to her late thirties, didn't deter him in the slightest.

For Fiamma, however, their romance posed certain complications. The Duchess had her aspirations; her eyes were set on a future in politics, a path where a relationship with an American military man didn't exactly fit. She wasn't ready to be tied down, especially not when her career was just about to take off.

A few days later, Mike returned to San Diego, heartbroken. His team was already there; They had been redeployed home following Mike's unplanned extended stay in Italy. With the memories of his brief, intense affair with the Duchess still fresh, He rejoined his men, carrying the experiences, lessons, and, frankly, the pain of his time in Rome.

Since her abrupt departure, Mike hadn't heard a word from the Duchess. She walked out of his life and never looked back. Now, there she was, standing right before him, just as stunning as he remembered. Caught off guard, He struggled to meet her gaze as Christina cheerfully introduced her new friend to her husband. The surprise of seeing her again stirred a whirlwind of emotions, bringing back memories he thought he'd left behind.

He nodded in acknowledgment, "Hello, Fiamma. It's nice to see you again."

The Prime Minister returned the gesture with a smile. "Yes, Michael, it is good to see you too. It has been a long time," she replied.

"It has. I see you've met my wife, Christina. This is my other wife..." He began but was quickly interrupted.

"Yes, Mike, the Prime Minister and I are acquainted. However, I didn't know you two knew each other. When did you meet?" Elena asked, her curiosity evident in her voice.

Christina, equally intrigued, was also keen to know the answer. She knew Mike's emotions better than anyone and could see that there was more to their interaction than met the eye. This revelation was not just intriguing to her; it was intoxicating.

He reluctantly replied, "The Duchess and I met when I was still in the Navy. Isn't that right, Madam Prime Minister?"

The Prime Minister answered with a measured response, "Sì, of course, we met in Rome if my memory serves me correctly. Just a brief encounter, as I recall."

Brief huh? Yeah right. I see that look in his eyes, Christina thought. She almost couldn't hold her tongue but found the strength to proceed with the ruse her husband was so obviously playing. "Well, it's good to meet you, Madam Prime Minister, and I am so honored we will be sitting at your table at the show tomorrow night. It's going to be awesome."

Mike quickly interjected," We are?"

Christina replied excitedly, "Yep! And best of all, it's right at the end of the runway. Oh my gosh, I'm so excited. Again, thank you, Madam..."

"Christina, please, call me Fiamma. We are like family—no need for such formalities. Now, if you three would excuse me, I must be going. Oh, there he is." Turning to Mike, she continued, "Michael, I believe you know my man, Marco. He is my head of security."

Marco gave a slight nod to Mike and the ladies as he approached. Mike smiled, instantly recognizing the man. They had just met in the kitchen, but Marco had not been dressed in the dark suit he was wearing now; he had been in a Head Chef's uniform.

"Yes, I do; hello, Marco. It's good to meet you," Mike replied, his smile masking the recognition of their earlier encounter.

Marco replied with professional courtesy, "Of course, Mr. McHaskell. Nice to formally meet you, as well."

"Michael, while you three are visiting my country, my man here will be at your service. Please do not hesitate to ask him for assistance with anything you might need. And Michael, understand that he will be with you the entire time," the Duchess informed, her nod conveying that his time in Italy would now be under close watch, far from the unencumbered freedom he had hoped for.

Huà Sūn:

"Good, you're awake," Christina remarked as she noticed Mike stirring. She had woken up early that morning and was hurrying to get ready and out the door. As Mike was stretching his side, she leaned over to give him a morning kiss.

"Sorry, I have to go; I wish I could stay a while with you this morning," she added, a hint of regret in her voice.

"It's okay, Sexy.... You're up early," he replied as he continued to stretch, his voice still heavy with sleep. "Hey, I'm sorry about last night. I was beat. I'll make it up to you tonight, I promise."

"Nonsense, Mike. We were both tired... I mean, we've been a bit busy for the last week," she replied playfully, winking at him. "And yes, I'll take you up on that offer tonight. But I really have to go." She collected the last of her things and leaned in to kiss him again. "Oh, I ordered you and Elena a nice breakfast. It will be here at 9:00. Why don't you get another hour of rest?"

Mike responded, "Sounds good. Have a good day, my love. I'm looking forward to seeing you on stage tonight."

Of course, he wasn't really looking forward to it. Since the moment he was informed of her modeling debut, Mike had been feeling extremely apprehensive. The idea of his wife, the love of his life, being on full display to the world wasn't something he was entirely comfortable with. But she was so excited, and that brought him happiness. So, in his mind, he relented, giving her the space to make her own decisions, albeit under the watchful eyes of her shadows.

When Christina emerged from the bedroom, Elena was seated at the living room table, sipping her coffee and reading the paper. Looking up, Elena commented, "You're up early, and ready to go, I see."

"Yep," Christina replied, a hint of distraction in her voice. "Hey, I just told Mike I ordered breakfast for you two. It will be here in an hour or so." She paused, something else clearly on her mind. "Elena, I'm sorry about last night, you know, getting out of the limo. Mike should have gone back for you. Really, I didn't know Lorenzo was going to be there to escort me, and the whole thing just got out of control. Again, it's my fault. I'm so sorry."

Elena chuckled lightly, brushing off the concern. "No, it's not, Christina. Don't worry yourself about such small things. I know you're Mike's world; we all do. It doesn't bother me."

"Elena, that's not true. Mike loves us all the same; it's just that sometimes he is a bit overprotective of me. Anyway, I'm truly sorry," Christina insisted, her tone earnest. She wanted to make sure Elena didn't feel overlooked or undervalued, especially given the complexities of their relationships.

Elena's reassurance was warm and understanding. "Look, Honey, really, it's fine. Mike and you have a special relationship, that's all. I'm not jealous. Actually, none of us are. We've discussed it, and it makes us happy that you two are so in love. I know how that sounds, but it's true."

Christina felt a pang of guilt. "Gosh, I wish you didn't think that way. I know he and I are sort of... Well, we're kind of co-dependent on each other. But really, I didn't want it this way. I feel bad. And now that you all think like this... Man, I don't know if that's a good thing or a..."

Elena interjected, her tone reassuring yet firm, "Christina, it's a good thing, really it is. Now you better get going, or you'll be late. Lorenzo's driver called; he's downstairs waiting for you."

Christina looked a bit worried, aware of the others' perceptions, as Elena had just confirmed, but she tried to shake it off, at least for the moment. However, another concern lingered in her mind, prompting her to ask, "Elena, Mike came to bed with his clothes on last night, a t-shirt and shorts. I know he was tired, but I mean, he never does that. It's like he was hiding something from me. Do you know what that was about? He told me he was just tired, and I want to believe him, but..." Her voice trailed off, filled with uncertainty and concern. This deviation from Mike's usual behavior seemed small, yet it was significant enough to her to cause worry. She sought reassurance or some insight from Elena, hoping to alleviate the uneasy feeling that had taken root in her mind.

"Don't worry too much about it; I'm sure he was just tired. Now, why don't you get going? I'm looking forward to tonight. It's going to be fun."

"Yeah, me too. Okay, see you tonight then," Christina replied with a half-smile, still a bit preoccupied as she walked out the door. Elena watched her leave, then made a quick phone call before returning to her reading.

A few moments later, Mike emerged from the bedroom. His body was sore, but he didn't mind. In fact, the feeling was somewhat satisfying. Hand-to-hand combat had always been something he enjoyed, as odd as that might sound. It had been missing from his life for a while, and though his sessions with Parker stirred up his dormant desires, he would never hurt his wife. Last night, his craving for a physical confrontation had been quenched, and this morning, he was content to pay the price for it.

"Good morning, Honey. How are you this fine day?" Mike greeted Elena, trying to sound upbeat despite the soreness that reminded him of the previous night's events.

"So you couldn't perform last night, I hear?" She laughed, egging her husband on.

Mike's expression shifted to one of amusement rather than annoyance. "Wow, that's quite the greeting. Good morning to you, too," he replied, playing along with Elena's light-hearted teasing.

"Haha! I'm just joking. Good morning, Mike. Here, I got you a coffee," she laughed, handing him a cup. Her tone then took a turn towards concern. "But seriously, Christina was worried about you, or should I say, your 'absence' last night. How messed up are you?"

The question, while posed with a hint of humor, carried a genuine concern. Elena's eyes scanned him, looking for signs of any physical distress.

He reassured her, trying to downplay his condition, "Not too bad, I think, only a couple of cracked ribs. A long way from my heart. I'll be fine."

Elena, however, wasn't having any of it and shook her head in exasperation. "You're such an idiot. Here, let me see, take off your shirt."

Reluctantly, he removed his shirt, revealing his right side, now mottled with shades of purple, blue, and yellow. "Oh my God, Mike, you might need to get this looked at. Wow, that has to hurt," she exclaimed.

"I'm fine," he insisted, trying to steer the conversation away from his injuries. "Christina mentioned something about breakfast?"

But Elena was not so easily diverted, "Mike, you are going to see the doctor." She picked up her phone and started to dial. He gently placed his hand over hers, stopping her mid-dial, and shook his head slowly.

"Honey, really, I'm okay," he insisted, trying to reassure her, though the evidence of his injuries suggested otherwise. This attempt to minimize his condition was typical of Mike, always the one to endure pain quietly.

"Fine, but if you get any worse, then we are going, and that's not a suggestion, Mike; it's an order," she asserted firmly, leaving no room for argument.

Mike smiled, acknowledging her concern, albeit half-heartedly, "Yes, my dear." He then asked, "And Christina? Did you call...?"

Elena quickly interjected, "Of course, my men are with her now. And your locals. By the way, who gave you permission to have me tailed? Like it or not, my husband, I am your superior here in Europe. Having me followed wasn't a good idea."

"My superior? Well, yes, you are at work, but you're still my wife. That makes you my top concern, Honey," Mike retorted, giving her his characteristic smirk, one that had the effect of a blend of irritation and charm on her.

Elena shook her head, a mixture of exasperation and affection in her response. "Fine, now sit. Bigs is on his way up. He has the intel you requested."

Biagio Caruso made his entrance with a rap at the door. He cut a striking figure, dressed in a suit that harked back to the 1950s – gray pinstriped, paired with white wingtips, and topped with a classic gray fedora. "Buongiorno amici, Elena e Mike. How are you this beautiful day?" he greeted them with a warm Italian flair.

"Buongiorno, Biagio. It's nice to see you," Elena replied cordially.

"Hey, Bigs. What do you have for me?" Mike asked, cutting to the chase.

"Wow, Michele, it's good to see you too," Bigs retorted, his tone playful yet hinting at reproach for Mike's abruptness.

Mike shook his head apologetically, "Sorry, man, I have a lot on my mind. Yes, hello, thanks for coming up."

"Ahhh, Certamente, capisco… Your Christina is the talk of the town. I thought that might be of concern to you. But my friend, don't worry. I have it on high authority she will be fine. In fact, the Duchessa herself has assigned her men to watch over her while you are here in Milan. Oh, by the way, did you know that Marco Forte, her head of security, is in the lobby?"

"Yeah, it seems that the Duchess has assigned him to me. We'll need to 'work' around him as best as possible," Mike replied, his mind already strategizing the best way to handle the presence of the Duchess's head of security.

Elena, discerning the implications in his expression, quickly intervened with a firm directive, "Mike, we do nothing to Marco, got it? I will talk to the Duchess if need be, but her man is off-limits. There's no way around that."

Turning to Biagio, she shifted the focus, "Okay, the floor is yours. What do you have for us?"

"Thank you, Chief," Bigs began. "So, Mike, your instincts were spot on. The General isn't here just for official work. Yes, that is part of his agenda, but it wasn't his true reason for being in Milan.

It seems he has a love interest at stake. His secretary, Ms. Huà Sūn. Scusi. Let me backtrack a bit. Ms. Sūn was his employee for the past ten years, working at the Ministry of State Security as his personal secretary. But as we all know, General Wu is married to Wei Yīngzhān, the influential sister of the Chinese President Mao Yīngzhān. Once Mrs. Wu learned about Ms. Sūn, the young secretary was promptly transferred out of the Ministry. She ended up here in Milan, working as an assistant to the Chinese ambassador's assistant—essentially hidden away. I believe the General is here to see her."

Mike's face lit up with intrigue. "So the General has an Achilles' heel. This Ms. Sūn, is she, let's say, accessible?"

Elena quickly interjected. "Mike, Sūn is a civilian. If anyone is to meet with her, it will be me. That's also non-negotiable," she stated firmly.

Turning her attention back to Biagio, Elena continued, "And where is the General staying, Bigs? Do we have that information?"

"Sì, Chief," Biagio, responded." The General has taken up residence next to the Chinese consulate, in an old brandy distillery—Casa d'Acquavite Lombardi. That place has been around for over a hundred years. The Chinese bought it for a song since the building not only reeks of booze, but it is not really usable for anything else. The Italian government considered it unlivable and slated it for destruction. But you know the Chinese—when they see a deal and have money to spend, they do not hesitate for a bargain."

Mike's mind began to churn, prompting him to ask more questions, "Bigs, tell me more about this building..."

Queen of the Nile:

Filling the day with mundane tasks proved to be torturous for Mike. Christina's intention for him and Elena to explore the city and strengthen their relationship was overshadowed by his overwhelming desire to be with Christina herself. The separation was more than he could bear. Even after their meeting with Caruso, as Mike began to devise a plan concerning the General, his thoughts incessantly drifted to his Christina—what she might be doing and with whom. Anyone familiar with the McHaskells, particularly Christina, would know she was not the type to indulge in the scenarios plaguing Mike's imagination. Deep down, he knew this, too, but his mind was clouded by an irrational grief.

This internal struggle was apparent in his actions, like how he was ready almost two hours before they were supposed to leave for the evening's event. Elena, perceptive and understanding, saw through his restlessness. She expedited her own preparations, readying herself as quickly as possible so they could arrive early.

"You guys are here already?" Christina asked, surprised as Elena entered the bustling dressing room backstage. Christina, amidst the chaos of models, fashion designers, photographers, and possibly even paparazzi, had a private dressing area. Yet, the space was hardly secluded, given the flurry of activity around her.

Elena replied, "Yes, Mike couldn't handle another minute away from you. But don't worry, he's sitting outside. I told him he couldn't come back here. But I said I would check on you and get back to him."

"Okay, I understand. Sorry for that. Oh, and he is wearing what I laid out for him, right?" Christina asked.

"Yes, of course, he is, and he looks fantastic."

"Great, thanks. Gosh, I hope he will be alright with me doing this tonight. I've been so nervous all day."

"Nonsense, Mike, and I support you in whatever you want to do. Besides, your makeup is terrific. I mean, awesome! They did an amazing job," Elena reassured her, turning the chair Christina was sitting on to get a better look. "And that jewelry, wow, that's nice. Is it gold?" she asked.

"Yes, it is, and you see those two men over there? The dark-haired guys," Christina motioned towards two men standing with their heads down, trying to avert their eyes from the models walking around in various states of dress.

"Yeah, who are they?"

"Well, they are from the Cairo Museum—all this jewelry, everything here. Wait, let me show you," Christina said, standing up.

She was covered from the neck down with a styling cape. As she removed it, Elena couldn't help but gasp. The sight of her friend in the most beautiful outfit she had ever seen was almost too much for her. "Oh my God, Christina, you look so amazing," she blurted out.

Lorenzo Cavallaro's latest collection, "Eredità del Mito," was a tribute to long ago, paying homage to the Pharaohs, Kings, and Emperors of the old world. Christina was adorned in an ensemble that could only be described as fitting for a queen. She embodied Cleopatra's Golden Phoenix, a magnificent sight from head to toe.

Starting at her head, she wore an intricately designed headdress worn by ancient Egyptian royalty. It was embellished with shimmering gold and lapis lazuli accents that framed her face beautifully, highlighting her features with regal elegance.

Her makeup was dramatic yet tasteful, with kohl-lined eyes and a bold gold eyeshadow that complemented the headdress. Her lips were painted in a deep, rich color, reminiscent of the luxuriousness of a bygone era.

The centerpiece of her attire was the iconic necklace—a stunning work of craftsmanship. It featured an array of fine gold links, leading to a large, exquisitely detailed phoenix pendant in the center. The phoenix, symbolizing renewal and grace, was encrusted with jewels that caught the light with every movement, making it a captivating focal point.

The dress itself was a masterpiece, flowing elegantly down her figure. Made of a sheer golden fabric, it was both revealing and semi-modest, with strategically placed elaborations adding to its allure. The material moved like liquid gold with each step she took, giving the impression of a walking, breathing piece of art.

Down to her toes, her feet were painted with delicate gold symbols, the design simple yet elegant, allowing the dress and the jewelry to take center stage. The entire ensemble was a perfect blend of historical opulence and modern fashion, making Christina not just a model on a runway but a walking embodiment of the Queen herself, the mighty Cleopatra.

"I know, right? This is the most beautiful thing I have ever seen. And Elena, all this stuff is real! I mean, the last time it was worn was by," she leaned in to whisper, "Cleopatra. Can you believe it? And the craziest part is, it all fits! I guess she and I are the same size. Look at this stuff."

A man entered the dressing room and announced in Italian, "People, five minutes to show. This is your five-minute call. All unauthorized persons must please return to their seats." As soon as the man left, Christina translated for Elena, "I'm sorry, but you have to go now. The show is starting."

"Yes, okay, Sweetheart. My gosh, Christina, I am so proud of you, and Mike will be too. Just have a great time, and we'll see you on the runway," Elena encouraged her warmly. The two women carefully hugged, ensuring they didn't alter Christina's ensemble, and said their goodbyes. Elena returned to Mike, who was craning his neck in an attempt to catch a glimpse of his Christina in the dressing room, though it was in vain.

"How is she? And your men?" He asked.

Elena answered, "Don't worry, Mike, she is fine. And yes, both are in position."

Moments later, with all his characteristic fanfare, Lorenzo Cavallaro made his way onto the stage. The venue was packed, every seat filled except for one—the Duchess's. Mike wondered to himself, *was she fashionably late? Or, hopefully, she has been called away for some reason.*

Truthfully, he hoped she would make an appearance. There were a few matters that needed clarification, issues Mike wasn't sure he was ready to confront but recognized needed to be addressed. Despite these concerns, his mind was preoccupied with seeing Christina, his anticipation overshadowing everything else.

"Signore e Signori, welcome to this year's Settimana della Moda. I am your host, Lorenzo Cavallaro. This evening, I aspire not just to dazzle your minds, but also to pay omaggio to the grand leaders of yesteryear. Tonight, I present to you the apice of years of dedizione, innumerable notti in bianco, and lacrime senza conto (pinnacle of years of dedication, innumerable sleepless nights, and countless tears). Witness my crowning achievement, 'Eredità del Mito.'" He clapped enthusiastically as he stepped aside, inviting the audience into the world of his creative vision.

One after another, beautiful women stepped forward, showcasing the fruits of Cavallaro's labor. Each gracefully walked the runway, pausing to strike a pose before continuing their elegant stride. It was a parade of artistry and beauty, yet Mike's attention was elsewhere. While he may have stolen a brief glance here and there, his gaze was primarily fixed on the back of the stage, where he anticipated Christina's arrival.

Elena, observing his focused anticipation, couldn't help but smile, understanding her husband's concerns. "Honey, she'll be up soon. Just relax," she reassured him gently. "Besides, look at this parade of almost naked bodies in front of you." Her comment, light and teasing, was an attempt to ease the tension and remind him to "enjoy" the spectacle unfolding before them.

Mike simply shrugged off Elena's comment, his gaze still unwaveringly fixed on the back of the stage.

"Buona sera, Elena, Michael. Mi scuso, for being so late," Prime Minister Fiamma Silenziosa greeted them politely before taking her seat. Mike only nodded in response, while Elena returned the greeting more warmly.

"I was afraid you might miss Christina. I think she's up next," Elena mentioned, aware of the Prime Minister's interest in seeing Christina's walk.

"Duty called, but thankfully, my assistant can handle it. Nothing too important," the Duchess replied. She then turned to Mike, observing the same intense focus that Elena had noted—his almost deathlike stare toward the back of the stage. "Michael, your beautiful Christina will be fine. She's special, that one. No need to worry," she reassured.

As the anticipation in the room reached its peak, Lorenzo Cavallaro stepped back onto the stage with a commanding presence. His eyes sparkled with excitement, mirroring the eager energy of the audience.

"Gente," he began, his voice resonating with enthusiasm and pride. "I am so deeply honored, or as we say in my native tongue, 'Mi è molto gradito,' for your wonderful reception of my collection thus far. But now, please prepare yourselves for the pinnacle of tonight's event, the crowning jewel of 'Eredità del Mito.'"

He paused, allowing the suspense to build, his gaze sweeping across the captivated crowd. "Questa sera, I have the distinct honor of introducing not only my masterpiece but also our newest spokeswoman. A woman who embodies the grace, power, and timeless beauty that this collection represents."

Cavallaro's voice rose in excitement. "Signore e Signori, please welcome the one and only Queen of the Nile, Cleopatra, brought to life by the stunning, the divina, Christina!"

The crowd erupted into applause, the energy in the room palpable. Lorenzo stepped aside, his expression one of immense satisfaction and anticipation, as all eyes turned towards the stage entrance, waiting for Christina's grand appearance. The moment was magical, special, and charged with a sense of historical grandeur, perfectly setting the stage for what was to come.

Suddenly, the room plunged into darkness, and a deep, rumbling sound resonated from strategically placed speakers. The vibration was so intense that it could be felt in the chests of all the onlookers. Then, the hisses of smoke machines filled the space, creating an ethereal atmosphere. Seconds later, strobes flickered, briefly illuminating the runway, followed by lasers moving at a dizzying pace. These rays revealed their true purpose as they converged to form a hologram, showcasing the magnificent moments of ancient Egypt in all their glory. As quickly as the light show had started, it ceased, leaving the audience in a brief moment of anticipatory silence.

The droning sound once again filled the air, accompanied by the familiar hiss of the smoke machines. Then, a flash of light zipped across the venue's ceiling, followed by another, momentarily drawing the patrons' attention away from the stage. This diversion was all part of the meticulously orchestrated plan.

As the lights gradually returned to the runway, Christina stood alone, striking the iconic pose of the Pharaohs. Unable to contain their excitement, the crowd erupted into cheers, yelling and screaming in awe at the truly unbelievable sight before them.

It was often said that the formidable Cleopatra wielded both her body and mind to exert control over her desires. The Queen was a consummate master of seduction, adeptly keeping the legendary Julius Caesar at bay for over two decades. Ultimately, she ensnared him with a dance—a dance of seduction that was as strategic as it was enchanting.

This composition of Cleopatra was more than a mere movement; it was a captivating display of grace and power. Each step she took was deliberate, her motions flowing like the Nile itself—smooth, commanding, and irresistibly enchanting. The air seemed to shimmer around her, her body swaying in rhythm with the haunting melody that filled the chamber. Her eyes sparkled with intelligence and allure, holding the gaze of all who watched, leaving them spellbound. The dance was not just a seduction of the body but of the mind, a mesmerizing blend of elegance, strength, and strategic charm that Cleopatra was renowned for. It was a performance that transcended time, leaving an indelible mark on the annals of history.

Christina had now become the embodiment of the great Queen, and the dance was hers to perform. As the music continued, she swayed slowly, her arms moving in perfect synchronization with the rest of her body. Each action captivated the audience, drawing every stare to her. However, her gaze was locked onto only one set of eyes—those that were the windows to her Mike's soul.

"Oh my God, she's so beautiful," he murmured, watching his wife slowly descend the runway. Even though there were hundreds of onlookers, for Mike, it felt as if only two people occupied the space. He was locked in a constant connection with the love of his life, mesmerized and utterly fascinated by her presence, savoring every moment of this spellbinding experience.

It was as though Cleopatra herself had graced the stage with her presence. Christina, manifesting the Queen with such authenticity and elegance, left everyone in awe. The men from Cairo, deeply immersed in the historical significance of the moment, each made a gesture of respect befitting royalty. With their right hands clenched into fists, they crossed them over their chests and bowed deeply to their Queen.

Time seemed to pause as Christina neared the end of the runway. Each step brought her closer to her mate, and as she did, a subtle smile graced her lips. In the climactic moment of her dance, she raised her hands above her head, and then, with dramatic flair, she abruptly stopped right in front of her husband. Seconds later, she gracefully dropped to her knees, arms outstretched, palms facing towards Mike. The music halted, and a bright spotlight pierced the darkness of the audience, focusing solely on the towering figure before her. In a powerful, resonant voice, she proclaimed, "My King!"

The audience, captivated by this theatrical display, burst into applause as Mike rose to meet his Queen. Unbeknownst to him, he was dressed in the feature presentation of the night's event—The Emperor Tuxedo, Lorenzo Cavallaro's latest masterpiece.

Markus you Really F$@#$ UP!:*

"Bailey, I don't care. Listen, Christina is mine, and not for sale!" Mike had called home to the Ranch. He left early for a meeting that morning, leaving Christina and Elena at breakfast under a flimsy pretext.

Bailey replied, "Mike, I understand, and I am sorry. I should have consulted you first…"

"Nonsense, Mike, you don't own OUR Christina; she is her own person. And for you to say something like that…" Parker, also on the call, couldn't contain her words. Being the household's self-proclaimed voice of reason when it came to women's rights, she felt compelled to speak up.

"Boston, I didn't mean it like that, and you know it. I just meant that I don't like being blindsided, that's all. Bailey, I'm sorry; I didn't mean to yell. But I do have a real problem with what happened last night."

Claire intervened, her voice calm and meditating, "It's okay, Mike. Everyone, let's just cool off. Parker, you're right. Mike, you need to think before you speak." She took a deep breath before continuing, "Now, Bailey, he does have a point. I wasn't aware of all that you had planned, either. I think this kind of thing should be discussed before we proceed, that's all. Mike, how about we discuss this when you two get home? Besides, Christina has a say in this, a big one. Wouldn't you all agree?"

Everyone on the call responded with various forms of agreement.

"I would just like to add—and I know it might not matter much—but, Mike, please let Christina know that Lorenzo called this morning, and from pre-orders alone, we have already made $20 million," Bailey responded in her typical matter-of-fact tone. It was her M.O., and everyone knew she often had trouble reading the room. If anyone else had made this comment, Mike might have come unglued, maybe justifiably so. However, he didn't react negatively this time. He loved his wife and understood her various social anomalies.

Recognizing the need to steer the conversation, Claire, who had been working with Bailey to help her understand the impact of her words, interjected once again, "Okay, Mike, you said you had something to do this morning? Let's just table this discussion for now."

Parker also chimed in, "Yes, that's a good idea. Mike, we'll see you when you get home."

"Okay, thank you, ladies. I miss you all so much and can't wait to see you. Please kiss my kids for me, and I'll see you soon."

He made his way towards La Dolce Sveglia. Earlier that morning, he received a text from Markus arranging a meeting concerning the General. However, as Mike approached, he was surprised to see two people he hadn't expected to be there.

Markus, with a smile that didn't quite reach his eyes, started the conversation. "Good morning, Mike. Have you read the paper today?" He tossed over the local newspaper. On the front page was a photograph of Christina as she made her proclamation. Markus continued, his tone laced with sarcasm, "Keeping a low profile, I see, MY KING!"

Not responding to Markus, Mike turned his attention to the other person sitting at the table. "Dad? Why are you here?" he asked with a mixture of surprise and curiosity.

Maximillian Sr, Mike's adopted father, was seated comfortably with a large plate of food in front of him. He was dressed casually in what looked like golf attire – a collared tee and shorts – giving the impression that he was on vacation.

"Hello, son, it's good to see you too," he replied."

"I didn't mean it like that, Dad. I... I'm just surprised to see you here, that's all," Mike quickly clarified. Turning back to Markus, "And why are you here, boss?"

Markus replied, "First, neither of us need to explain ourselves to you. Second, I told you I had someone who could come and help with your Mission."

Mike appeared confused as he mentioned Elena's presence. "Markus, you sent Elena to help. She's with Christina now at the hotel restaurant."

Markus's expression of confusion mirrored Mike's, intensifying as he asked, "Chief Alvarez is here?"

"Yes, brother, you sent her here, didn't you?"

Markus paused momentarily, his mind racing to piece together who was responsible for this unexpected development. A realization dawned on his face, yet he chose not to share the full extent of his understanding with Mike. "Of course I did. It was a long flight; I guess I'm more tired than I thought. Anyway, let's get down to business, shall we?"

Mike turned his attention back to his father, who began to speak with a serious tone. "Son, take a seat. Markus and I have something to tell you, and knowing how you feel about your wives, It might not be so well received."

As Max and Markus began to recount their time together in Afghanistan, years before Mike had worked in the same territory, Mike's eyes narrowed, curiosity and apprehension evident in his expression.

"Markus, I know you worked with the team and my dad. So, why are you bringing this up now?" he asked, his voice tinged with confusion and a hint of suspicion.

Max Sr. asked, "Son, do you remember my teammate Chris Canepa? He was my assistant coach for your and Max's baseball team."

Mike nodded in affirmation. Max then gestured towards Markus, signaling him to continue the conversation.

"Mike, first, I need you to listen to the entire situation before you react. Senior Chief Canepa, your father, and I..." Markus began, his tone indicating the seriousness of what he was about to reveal.

He went on to explain everything that had transpired. Markus detailed the Mission, the unexpected complications that arose, and, most significantly, the death of the man who would have been Mike's father-in-law. As he delved deeper into the story, Markus eventually reached the crux of the matter – the request the Senior Chief had made of him.

This part of the narrative was where Markus had anticipated the strongest reaction, and true to his expectations, Mike was about to come unglued. This story was delivered in a public setting for everyone's protection. Like it or not, he would have to control his inner beast in such an open place. His response was intense, a mix of emotions clearly playing out as he processed the revelations about his past and the people closest to him.

"What the FUCK, Markus!" he slammed his fist on the table, "Where the hell were you? She needed you to protect her, so where were you?" Mike's voice, filled with anger and frustration, echoed across the courtyard, affecting everyone within earshot.

Max Sr., sensing the need to intervene, spoke up firmly, "Son, that's enough. You don't know the entire story. Just listen. Alright?" His words, though calm, carried an authority that demanded attention.

However, only one person on earth had the power to soothe the tumultuous storm brewing that was Mike, and she wasn't there. His eyes turned as dark as a starless night sky. His face became set in stone; his gaze, which only a very unlucky few had ever seen, was now squarely focused on the Director. "Markus, do you understand what those girls went through? How their lives have been forever changed? It was only by sheer luck that I was there. My God, Markus, think about it. If anything had been different – if I had been sent to another CAGE, or if they had been..." his voice trailed off, laden with the weight of what might have been.

Max Sr. interjected his tone both understanding and firm. "Son, I know what you're thinking, and yes, things could have been different. It's only by the grace of God that they worked out as they did. But, son, they did. And I love my daughters-in-law, my grandbabies, and your life. I feel your pain, and I understand how angry you are. But things worked out as they should have. And I wouldn't change any of it if I could."

Markus added, his voice tinged with genuine regret, "Mike, I know I messed up. I really did. I have no excuse. I can only hope you, Claire, and Christina can forgive me. That Chris, looking down, can forgive me. This is a cross I will bear for the rest of my life, my brother. I am truly sorry."

Mike was momentarily speechless, lost in his thoughts. He was acutely aware that things could have been different, and sometimes, he wondered if the girls would have had a better life if they were. He had often questioned himself, pondering if they would have been better off without him, and had reluctantly concluded that they might have been. Now, hearing that things could have, and perhaps *should* have been different and that it was Markus's fuck up that led to this situation, he was overcome again with remorse for the lives they should have had without him.

After a few moments of thought, he turned to his father. He found himself unable to meet Markus's gaze, the revelation too fresh and raw. Instead, he directed his question, seeking answers that might help him make sense of it all. "Dad, when did you know?" he asked.

Max Sr., choosing his words with care, responded, "When you three returned from Saudi, as soon as she walked off the plane, I knew... Those eyes, son, and that smile. It was as if Chris was there, in front of me again. Now listen, Mike, your mother and I love Christina. She is our daughter, and again, I wouldn't change anything for the world."

Markus felt it was necessary to try to explain the situation, even though he knew it could not change anything. He acknowledged his mistakes but believed it was important to clarify. "Mike, after Chris died, Christina's mother wanted nothing to do with us, the military, or me. I tried, I really tried. But she wanted me out of her life, and truthfully, I don't blame her. A few years later, she moved back to her family's home in Ohio. Married a good guy who had a daughter of his own, and went on to raise them into really great young ladies. Like I said, this isn't an excuse. But need it to be heard."

"He's right, son. Telling Valentina about Chris was one of the hardest things I had to do. She looked at me with such disdain, and like Markus, I deserved it. We thought it best to let her go, and that's what we did. Looking back, it was the correct decision."

Mike realized he needed a moment to himself to cool off and process everything. Markus was like family, and although he had questions that needed answering, he knew deep down that Markus would be safe from any serious repercussions coming from him. His dad had a point—Mike's life was more than he could have ever dreamed of. Maybe, in some way, Markus had contributed to that. Yet, despite this acknowledgment, he was too upset to continue sitting and discussing it with his boss, a man he thought of as a brother. He needed space to sort this out, to work the problem. "Guys, I need to get my head around this. I'll be back," he said, standing up swiftly and moving out of sight.

Markus turned to Max Sr. with concern etched on his face. "Do you think he'll be alright? We're in this now and need to get the job done."

Max Sr. replied confidently, "Yes, Markus. Mike will come around. We've got Claire to help with that. Now, onto the next thing, brother. You need to tell Christina about her father. It's something you have to do."

"I know," Markus replied, letting out a deep sigh, his demeanor reflecting the weight of the task ahead. "It's going to be one of the most difficult conversations I've ever had. But yes, you're right; it needs to be done." He picked up his phone and called Elena. A few moments later, a meeting was arranged. Elena had a matter to "attend" to first, but afterward, she would escort Christina to meet them, paving the way for Markus's sincere conversation with her.

Swallowing deeply, he nodded to Max Sr., indicating his resolve. "Okay, it's set."

Gli Appartamenti Del Circolo Tennistico:

"Christina, please hurry up. Mike could return any second," Elena called out.

The two women were preparing for a rendezvous, but not in the traditional sense. Elena's newest subject, not exactly what she would call a Target, required a delicate approach, and Christina had offered to help. Elena couldn't put her in any danger, of course, but she could utilize Christina's assistance in surveillance.

Her plan was to enter the apartment of Ms. Huà Sūn while she was at work. There, Elena intended to initiate the next phase of her plan. The Chinese president was adamant that *"Ms. Sūn has no contact with General Wu."* Therefore, Sūn and the General had resorted to using a series of cryptic messages sent through various apps. These were crafted to be nearly impossible for the Chinese government to decipher, assuming they were even aware of their existence.

However, as a Chinese citizen and an employee at the Chinese consulate in Milan, Huà Sūn's right to privacy was limited. Her phone and any personal electronic devices were subject to search while on consulate property. Therefore, she would likely leave such items at her apartment, off government property. This placed her under the jurisdiction of the Italian government, where she enjoyed a greater degree of privacy. It was this vulnerability that Elena planned to exploit.

Christina emerged from the bedroom, smiling and eager. "Okay, I'm ready," she announced cheerfully.

Elena couldn't help but raise an eyebrow as she asked, "What in the hell are you wearing?"

"What? I think I look cute, don't I?" Christina replied, turning around slowly with her hands on her hips to showcase her outfit.

"Yes, very cute, but I told you we need to keep a low profile. This," Elena motioned up and down at her, "isn't low profile."

"Wait, you told me we were going to a Tennis Club. I thought my tennis whites would be the best thing to blend in," Christina explained, a hint of confusion in her voice.

"My God... No, Christina. I said we were going to the Tennis Club Apartments. Whatever, let's just get going," Elena replied, raising her arms in mild exasperation as she turned toward the door.

"Well, I think I look great anyway," Christina retorted with a hint of playfulness, following closely behind.

The ride to the apartments was unusually quiet for Christina. She remained mostly silent, which Elena found odd. Christina could talk just to hear the sound of her own voice. While she appreciated the peace, curiosity nudged her to break the silence. "Okay, what's going on in that head of yours? I can tell you're thinking about something. Spill it?" she prompted.

Christina took a deep breath before voicing what had been preoccupying her mind. "Elena, don't take this the wrong way. I love you, and you know that. But... how old are you, exactly? I know, I'm sorry to ask, but looking at you now... And believe me, you are beautiful, truly beautiful. I'm still in awe, but..." she trailed off again into silence, leaving her question hanging in the air.

Elena's face briefly showed a flicker of rage as she responded, "What the hell are you talking about, little miss? You know exactly how old I am..." She paused, gearing up to continue her retort, but then she realized why Christina had asked. In her efforts to blend in for the day's operation, she had altered her makeup and style significantly.

For Elena, her beauty often posed a challenge in covert operations. In her line of work, the goal was to be a face in the crowd—unnoticed and unmemorable. Elena's striking appearance, while a source of pride, had also been a hindrance in her career. In fact, her looks and physique had almost been a barrier to her joining the CIA. However, with practice, Elena had mastered the art of altering her appearance to diminish her natural allure, allowing her to blend in seamlessly with the general faceless populace. This skill was especially crucial today, as she needed to enter the apartment building without drawing attention to herself.

Now, with a laugh, she continued, "Haha, yes, my makeup. Well, like I wanted you to, I changed my appearance to blend in. That's why I asked you to get ready and wear something not so..." She glanced up and down at Christina again, her amusement evident. "Wait. Why would you pack a tennis outfit for this trip? I mean, you're heading to Milan, and you think, 'Gosh, I wonder if we're going to play tennis?'"

"Hey, you can never be too prepared. That's my motto, anyway," Christina replied, her tone light and playful as she returned to staring out the window in silence.

My gosh, our poor Mike, Elena thought to herself.

Moments later, having left her security detail at the corner coffee shop with strict instructions to stay put, the two approached the front doors of the apartment building.

The Tennis Club Apartments, loosely translated from "Gli Appartamenti del Circolo Tennistico," was a relatively new building in the area. Contrary to what its name might have suggested, it had no actual connection to the sport—there were no courts for miles. Nevertheless, residing in this building was a status symbol. It represented modern luxury, a stark contrast to the more historic and vintage dwellings typically found in Milan. Such places were rare in this city steeped so deeply in history.

It was no surprise, then, that someone like Huà Sūn, accustomed as she was to the high-class and sophisticated apartments of Beijing, would choose this particular building as her residence in Milan. The Tennis Club Apartments offered a slice of contemporary opulence that appealed to her, "more refined tastes."

In light of its high-class status, the building was equipped with a doorman, security guards, and, of course, video surveillance. This was where Christina's role would be crucial.

Elena, pointing towards the doors, laid out the plan. "Okay. So, I need you to be a distraction. There are three of them—the doorman and two guards. First, get the doorman away from the door, then engage all of them in a discussion. After I slip by, you leave. Get out of there and head back to the coffee shop," she instructed, her tone serious.

She then held Christina by the shoulders, emphasizing the importance of the next part. "Listen, you head straight back to my men, got it? I mean it, Christina, do as I ask."

Christina nodded in understanding. "Yes, I got it," she replied, but a concern lingered in her mind. After a moment's pause, she voiced her worry, "But what about you? What if they catch you... or what if the woman comes home?"

"Don't worry about me; I'll be fine. Your job is to follow the plan and stay safe. Just do as you're told, okay? Now, let's get going."

It took only a few seconds for the doorman to become mesmerized by Christina's 'extremely short' tennis outfit and her 'blue eyes,' enhanced by her larger-than-life smile. Soon after, both of the guards were equally captivated. Elena watched Christina work her magic, a smile on her face and a shake of her head in mild disbelief at the scene unfolding before her. Christina was in her element, laughing and lightly touching each man's shoulder, incapacitating them with her charm and natural charisma. It was a flawless execution of distraction, allowing the assassin the perfect opportunity to slip by unnoticed.

Once inside Huà Sūn's apartment, Elena immediately got down to business. Though she had told Christina she was just looking for a phone or computer, her real objective was something else entirely. Yes, searching for electronic devices was part of her plan, but Elena had done her research—or, more accurately, her assistant back in Paris had.

Huà Sūn was a diabetic, requiring insulin multiple times a day. Insulin needs refrigeration to maintain its efficacy. When Elena opened the refrigerator, she found exactly what she was looking for: Huà Sūn's weekly insulin supply. Elena knew that Sūn would carry her daily dose with her, but the stash in the fridge was what she needed for the evening, now conveniently within her reach.

Sūn, unlike many diabetics who use an insulin pen, relied on an insulin pump. This device, which required daily refilling, held just enough insulin for her needs while at work. Each day at 5 pm, the unit needed to be refilled with fresh medication.

Elena, the silent assassin, executed her plan with precision. She carefully swapped one of the glass insulin vials in the fridge with another she had brought in her pocket. Unlike Mike, whose methods were more 'hands-on,' Elena adhered to a traditional role in her occupation, aligning with the methods preferred by the Agency.

With this switch, the trap was set. Once Sūn replaced her exhausted supply with the tampered bottle Elena had planted, her fate would be sealed. This seemingly innocuous act would unknowingly lead to her demise, a grim yet calculated move in the complex game of espionage.

The job was complete. Christina should have been back at the coffee shop by now, and Huà Sūn would unknowingly fulfill the rest of Elena's plan. Yet, things didn't unfold as expected.

First, Christina hadn't left the building. While engaging the doorman and guards in conversation, she noticed an Asian woman entering the lobby. Not knowing what Huà Sūn looked like, she followed her movements discreetly and saw her enter the elevator—the same one Elena had used just minutes before. When Christina finally managed to disengage from the conversation with the men, she quickly retrieved her phone to warn Elena about the potential complication.

However, time was not on their side. Moments later, Elena heard the unmistakable sound of keys entering the lock of the apartment door. Then, as the door swung open, she found herself face-to-face with Huà Sūn. The unexpected arrival turned the situation on its head, leaving Elena to swiftly adapt to the unforeseen turn of events. *Alright, I guess we do this now*, she thought to herself.

Like many individuals in Sūn's previous line of work, she was trained in hand-to-hand combat and maintained a constant state of vigilance, always prepared for the possibility of facing a friend or foe. Now, confronted with the sight of an unexpected intruder in her apartment, her instincts kicked in, and she immediately assumed the worst—a conclusion that, in this instance, was accurate.

Reacting quickly, Sūn reached for her hidden weapon, a concealed CZ 75 handgun, which she had discreetly placed in a drawer in the entrance table to her right. Her actions were swift and precise.

Elena, equally trained and prepared for such a confrontation, quickly responded. She executed a powerful roundhouse kick to Sūn's left arm, momentarily stunning her opponent. This brief window of opportunity allowed Elena to ascertain what Sūn was reaching for. With deft movements, she secured the firearm before Sūn could utilize it.

Sūn was not one to concede easily. She quickly regained her stance and struck Elena on the right side, causing the sidearm to fly from Elena's grasp and land under a glass table in the living room.

The fight intensified as the two women, both highly trained in combat, found themselves locked in a struggle for survival. Their movements were a deadly dance of attack and defense, each vying for the upper hand in a battle that would end when the life of one woman was extinguished.

In a strategic move, Elena grabbed a vase of roses from the living room side table and struck Sūn in the face. Slivers of porcelain sketched a trail of cuts across Sūn's cheek, a testament to the intensity of their struggle.

Sūn quickly retaliated, seizing a glass ashtray from the coffee table and hurling it toward her adversary. However, Elena's reflexes allowed her to narrowly avoid a direct hit, deflecting the solid projectile milliseconds before it could impact her left eye.

In that brief moment of distraction, as Elena was still recovering from the ashtray's near miss, Sūn spotted her firearm, now lying inconspicuously beneath the table. Seizing the opportunity, she lunged for the CZ 75, determined to regain control of the situation. Her movements were precise, driven by the urgency of the fight.

Elena, quick to notice Sūn's intent and the direction of her lunge, acted swiftly. She leaped forward, grabbing Sūn just as she reached for her weapon. The combined weight of the two women was too much for the glass coffee table to bear. It shattered dramatically, sending shards of glass flying through the air as they both hit the ground with a heavy thud.

Despite the disorienting fall, Sūn's resolve remained unshaken. Her hand found its target amidst the chaos. Though somewhat dazed from the impact, she now held her prized savior—the CZ 75—firmly in her right hand.

Elena found herself at a distinct disadvantage, her fate seemingly sealed as she and Huà Sūn slowly stood from the shattered remnants of the coffee table. Sūn, her face smeared with blood, wore a triumphant smile as she took aim. For Elena, time appeared to slow down, each second stretching out as she braced for what seemed like her inevitable end.

Just then, in a twist of fate, the front door burst open, and Christina charged in. Her only weapon was a bottle of CS gas, snatched from one of the security guards. She began to spray it at Sūn, who held her Elena at gunpoint. However, Sūn, well-trained for such situations, wasn't fazed. She even laughed off the attempt, her aim now shifting to Christina, the new threat rapidly approaching her.

Sūn's momentary distraction proved to be her final mistake. The first rule in combat; "never turn your back on an adversary." Elena, seizing this crucial opportunity, quickly spotted a sharp, jagged shard of glass, a remnant of the now-destroyed table. With a swift, decisive movement, she grabbed the improvised weapon and, in one fluid motion, plunged it deep into Huà Sūn's neck.

The action was sudden and precise, hitting its mark with deadly accuracy. Blood spurted out like a fountain as Huà Sūn's heart began to race, pumping furiously in her final moment. Within mere seconds, the intense entanglement came to a decisive end. Elena stood over the lifeless body of her Target, her survival instincts having guided her through the lethal confrontation.

Before she could fully process the aftermath, another sound caught her attention—a second body hitting the ground. Turning, she saw Christina, who had collapsed, unconscious from the overwhelming and gruesome scene that had just unfolded before her.

"Jesus," Agent Joe Harvey, peering through the scope of his McMillan TAC-338, couldn't help but react. His finger, which had been tensed on the trigger, now slowly lifted away, the shot he was about to take no longer necessary. Joe and two others were perched atop the roof of the opposing building, providing overwatch. Unbeknownst to Elena, her Mission was under constant surveillance. "Mike's got a knack for choosing 'em, that's for sure," he remarked. "Jack, make the call, we're green. Huà Sūn is no longer of any concern."

Agent McHaskell I Need a Word!:

"Agent McHaskell, I need a word!"

Markus Delphy, the Director of the Central Intelligence Agency, was on the phone, reaching out across the globe to the States. After Mike's abrupt departure, he and Max Sr. returned to their hotel. Which, incidentally, was the same one where Mike and the women were staying. In a strategic move, the two men had taken up residence in Elena's unused room, positioning themselves at a vantage point close to the heart of their ongoing operation. More accurately, their choice of location was primarily to keep a watchful eye on Mike.

"Hello, Markus. How are you today?" Claire responded, her voice carrying a note of preparedness. She had a hunch about the reason for Markus's call and was ready for the conversation that was about to unfold.

Over the past few months, the Director had assigned his top Codebreaker to a covert task. Claire's Mission was to oversee and monitor certain individuals within the Agency, scrutinizing digital and analog communications for any discrepancies.

Claire possessed a unique talent for pattern recognition, a skill crucial in Counterintelligence Operations. Although most processes in this domain focused on similar goals, their techniques varied significantly. The Counter Intelligence Mission Center, or CIMC, relied heavily on complex computer algorithms designed to detect anomalies in communications. This system was primarily effective with digital data.

Claire had proven her capabilities beyond these digital confines, outperforming the supercomputer on multiple occasions. Her ability to see patterns where algorithms faltered made her an invaluable asset. Consequently, she had become Markus's go-to expert in this regard, trusted for her exceptional skills in unraveling complex information puzzles.

After a period of upheaval, often described as the Agency "removing the dead flesh" from its war-torn body, Markus was determined to prevent a recurrence of such turmoil. With the CIA now under his leadership, he was resolute in ensuring that nothing would again jeopardize the integrity of his domain. To facilitate this, he tasked Claire with identifying anyone who might be involved in activities that could threaten the Agency's stability. She was to pinpoint potential threats; after that, CIMC would take over to either exonerate or "resolve" the issues with the officers in question. Claire was not informed about the specific outcomes of these investigations, but she had a fair idea of what they entailed.

She approached her new role with the utmost seriousness. Initially, she identified only a few individuals requiring closer scrutiny as per Markus's directive. However, Claire didn't limit herself to these names alone. She adopted a more comprehensive, "sweeping" approach, delving much deeper than what was explicitly asked of her. In doing so, she uncovered information and secrets that, in hindsight, she might have preferred not to know. Despite the regret that some of these revelations brought, Claire persisted, driven by her commitment to duty and the greater good of the Agency.

"First of all, when *exactly* did I give you permission to access my personal data, including my emails and letters?" the Director asked, his tone edged with anger and sternness.

Understanding the delicate nature of the situation, Claire chose her words very carefully in response to the Director's stern question. "Mr. Director, yes, I might have seen a few things. But I'm not sure why you would be so upset. It was in your order...."

Before she could finish her explanation, Markus interrupted, his voice carrying a blend of irritation and an undefinable emotion. "Claire, don't try to outsmart me. Yes, you are good at what you do, but I am better. I explicitly told you not to go where you weren't authorized."

"You did, and I am sorry, Markus. I overstepped. I know it's no excuse, but I just got lost going down the rabbit hole. I am truly sorry."

Markus's frustration was palpable, "Claire, I don't want to hear it," he said, his patience clearly worn thin. His star pupil, whom he had trusted implicitly, had exceeded her boundaries in ways he couldn't have foreseen.

He pressed on, his words laced with a sense of betrayal. "So it all makes sense now. The tickets for Mike and Christina you *recommended* I buy when I sought your advice. How Alessandro's 'find,' something so minor, ended up on my desk. Then, there's General Wu's coincidental presence in Milan... at the same time as Mike. And, of course, Mike finds out and predictably loses it. And, out of nowhere, Elena showed up, and I did not authorize any of that. It was all orchestrated by you..."

His voice rose in intensity, "God damn it, Agent McHaskell, you do not set Missions or run Ops! You are *way* out of your lane."

Claire remained silent for a moment, contemplating her response. There was a heaviness in the air, a tension that reflected the gravity of the moment. When she finally spoke, her voice was calm but firm.

"Markus, when I discovered that email from you to my father-in-law... When I learned about what happened to Christina's father and that you and Dad were there—and by the way, I am truly sorry for what both of you went through—I felt compelled to act. I'll admit, my approach might have been a bit overboard. But you have to understand, it seemed necessary, at the time. Looking back, I'm glad I did what I did, even if it means our relationship and my standing with the Agency might be compromised."

Markus's voice was full of disbelief and exasperation. "Compromised! You think you might only be compromised? Claire, you could be thrown in jail for this. And if this situation spirals any further out of control, we could be looking at an international crisis. For God's sake, maybe even World War III! Do you have any idea of the potential shitstorm you've set in motion with your actions?" He paused, his frustration at its limits.

"You and Mike are more alike than you realize. He's exactly the kind of person who would pull a stunt like this," he said, drawing parallels between Claire's actions and Mike's known tendencies for unilateral decision-making.

Then, a sudden realization hit him, his thoughts racing as he pieced together the enormity of what had transpired. "How did you even come up with this plan? I know you have access to major intel, but you don't have any influence in China. To orchestrate the General's movement, handle all the logistics here, and even involve the Prime Minister of Italy..." he rubbed his temple, a new suspicion dawning in his mind. "Yeah, Claire, this isn't something you could have managed on your own. Who is really behind this?"

His question hung in the air, suggesting a deeper conspiracy at play, one that extended well beyond Claire's capabilities.

Her response was brief, yet it carried a weight that extended beyond the mere words spoken. "Markus, I am sorry, but I am not able to provide you with the answer to your question. Just rest assured, no international incident will come to pass. On that, you have my word."

I Want You To Take This With You:

Today marked one of the most emotional days in Christina's relatively short life. After returning to the hotel with Elena, they were met by Markus, who appeared agitated and urgently requested a private conversation with her.

From her vantage point on one of the hotel lobby's plush couches, Elena observed the two talking. She watched as Christina's expression shifted from her usual cheerfulness to a visage marred by pain and sorrow. The transformation was gradual but unmistakable.

Moments later, in a gesture laden with significance, Markus reached into his jacket pocket and handed something to Christina. The object, whatever it was, seemed to trigger a profound emotional response in her, and she broke down into uncontrollable sobs.

Max Sr. approached Elena from behind as she intently observed the unfolding scene. Startled, she greeted him, "Dad, hey, I didn't know you were here?"

Max Sr. responded with warmth, leaning in to hug and kiss his daughter-in-law. "Hello, Honey," he said softly. There was a certain heaviness in his voice as he continued, "Markus is telling our Christina about..." His voice trailed off, indicating the gravity of the news being shared and the impact it was having on everyone involved.

Elena, unaware of the details surrounding Christina's father, was caught off guard by the emotional scene before them. Had she been privy to this sensitive information, she might have cautioned Markus that today was already quite challenging for Christina due to their earlier "activities." However, Markus had simply requested a meeting with Christina and hadn't divulged any further details to Elena.

Sensing the need to provide comfort, Max Sr. gently moved close to his young daughter-in-law. His actions were those of a caring and concerned father figure, instinctively stepping in to offer support and solace in her time of emotional distress. Christina welcomed the effort and quickly burrowed into his chest.

As Mike roamed the bustling streets of Milan, he hoped to shake off the thoughts that plagued him, seeking a brief respite from the turmoil in his mind. Despite his initial efforts to clear his head, much of his day inevitably turned to conducting recon on the Casa d'Acquavite Lombardi building.

He was meticulous in his observations, carefully noting every detail that would be crucial for the night's Mission. Forming a strategic plan, he assessed entry points, security measures, and potential obstacles, all the while blending (almost) seamlessly into the city's vibrant atmosphere. After gathering all the necessary intel, he made his way back to the hotel room.

Christina had returned to the suite about an hour earlier, visibly exhausted and emotionally drained. The combination of the day's events, along with the early stages of her pregnancy, had taken a significant toll. Overwhelmed by the myriad of emotions and physical discomfort, she had cried herself to sleep in the couple's bed, seeking solace in the quiet and privacy of the room.

Considering Christina's state and respecting her need for rest and privacy, Elena chose not to return to the suite. The hotel was a safe place; she had ensured that and decided it would be more prudent to focus on the upcoming evening's task. She opted to go over the plan that Markus and Max Sr. were developing. Heading to their room, she prepared to delve into the details of their strategy, understanding the importance of being fully aligned and prepared for what lay ahead.

Mike's return to the room was greeted by his Christina's soft, sweet voice, barely audible from beneath the blankets. "Your back," she murmured, her words tinged with relief and weariness.

He approached the bed, his concern for her evident in his tone. "Yes, my love, I'm back. How are you? Markus told me he talked with you. Are you okay?" he asked gently.

Christina propped herself up, making an effort to meet her husband with a tender kiss. "I'm okay," she began, her voice carrying a softness tinged with melancholy. "I didn't know my father, so I never really mourned his death. My dad loved Claire and me so much that I never felt I was missing out. But today, I guess... well, I just feel sad, that's all. Just really sad."

Mike's response was filled with empathy. "That's understandable, Honey," he said, offering comfort. "You were just blindsided by our friend. So was I," he added.

Christina, seeking a deeper connection to the past she never knew, turned to him with a question of longing. "Mike, you knew my father. What was he like?" she asked, her eyes searching his for answers.

He smiled warmly, a hint of nostalgia in his eyes. "Well, Christina, I was just a kid when I met the Senior Chief... I mean, your father. But I do remember him. He was a really good guy, you know," he chuckled softly, the memory bringing a lightness to the moment. "I remember this one time he was helping Dad coach our baseball team. Poor Max just couldn't get the hang of catching grounders. So your dad, with that classic sense of humor of his, told him that if he kept missing shots even his grandmother could catch, the girls watching would never... well, you know,.... with him. Babe, I've never seen my brother so motivated to up his game. It was hilarious."

The anecdote brought a smile to his love's tear-stained face, lightening the mood momentarily. She looked at him with curiosity and a hint of hopefulness. "Is that all you remember? I do realize you were young, but is that everything?"

Mike's expression softened, reflecting a blend of regret and understanding. "I don't know... really, Honey, I just didn't know him that well. I'm really sorry; I wish there was more I could tell you."

"Ohh, that's alright. Maybe you'll remember something else someday," she said, her eyes scanning the room briefly before settling back on Mike. "About tonight, can we just stay in? I know we have tickets for the show and all, but I'm tired. Maybe we can order room service? I don't know where Elena is, but we can get something for her too." She paused for a second before continuing, "Sorry, but I'm just too exhausted and don't want to get out of bed. I hope you're not upset," she added.

Mike felt a surge of relief at her suggestion, which perfectly aligned with his own plans for the evening. He had a Mission to complete that night, and keeping Christina in the room was an integral part of his strategy. Initially, he had planned to coax her back to the room after dinner for some alone time, during which he would execute his plan to leave unnoticed.

Her preference for a quiet night in was an unexpected but welcome twist, making things significantly easier for him.

He quickly responded, eager to reassure her, "Of course, Babe, whatever you want. And don't worry about Elena; she's out with Markus and Dad tonight. They wanted to give us a night alone." He smiled, a new plan forming in his mind. "I'll order up something great, my love."

After enjoying their meal together, Christina's energy levels dipped once again. Despite her earlier contemplation of venturing out to the "cute little place" next door for some gelato and hot chocolate, her exhaustion prevailed.

With a yawn that seemed to echo her day's weariness, she suggested, "Maybe we could go back to the bedroom and snuggle?" Her voice was soft, signaling her readiness to end the day with some quiet, comforting moments in the embrace of her husband.

Mike, however, had pressing "matters" that required his attention – things Christina was unaware of. Seizing the opportunity, he quickly concocted an excuse to stay behind a little longer. "I'll just finish watching the game, then I'll be right in," he assured her, masking his true intentions.

As soon as Christina drifted off to sleep, Mike made his move. He tried to slip out of the hotel room swiftly and silently. Making his departure seamless, leaving no trace of his exit, as he set off to "execute" the Mission that awaited him.

Caught in the act, he froze as Christina's unexpectedly alert voice reached his ears. "Mike, where are you going?"

He turned around slowly, his mind racing to concoct a plausible excuse. Yet, he was momentarily at a loss for words, realizing that Christina had sensed he was up to something. Something he hadn't intended to share with her.

Christina's expression conveyed a deep concern, her voice cracking with emotion, "I know you need to go out tonight, and I understand. I'm just worried about you. I can't lose you, Mike, I just can't." Her tears returned, though she tried to regain composure, her vulnerability palpable in the dimly lit room.

In response, Mike's instinct was to comfort her. He walked towards her with outstretched arms, enveloping her in a reassuring embrace. He kissed her gently, "Babe, I will be back, I promise you. I love you too, sweetheart, and I will never leave you. You have my word," he assured her, his voice steady and full of resolve.

Christina couldn't help but crack a small smile through her worries. She trusted that he would come back if he could; it was the scary thought that maybe one day he couldn't that was freaking her out. Today had been a real eye-opener for her. She always had an idea of what Mike's "job" involved, but after what went down with her and Elena, it hit her hard how dangerous his world really was. It was a harsh truth she wished she hadn't learned, but now it was right in front of her, clear as day.

She reached into her pocket and pulled out something given to her earlier. With a gentle hand, she placed it into his. "Mike, I want you to carry this with you, then bring it back to me when you are finished," she said softly, without meeting his gaze.

It was unusual for her not to look directly at him while speaking. It wasn't that she didn't want to see his face; on the contrary, she yearned to look at him. But right then, she couldn't bear the thought of reading any sign or expression that might hint he wouldn't fulfill his promise to return to her. She wanted to hold onto hope without the burden of additional fears.

After giving him a tight squeeze, affirming her love and worry in that single embrace, Christina turned back towards the bedroom. Her voice was tender yet heavy with emotion as she said, "I love you, Mike, and I always will. Nothing could ever change that. You... are my everything," she quietly closed the bedroom door behind her.

My God, That Woman is Diabolical:

"Of course, Sir, I fully understand," Markus responded, his voice steady despite the discomfort the call was causing him. "Yes, Sir, I agree. However, being in the loop beforehand would certainly have helped... Yes, I understand, Sir. I assure you the situation will be handled promptly. You have my word," he continued.

This conversation with the White House was unexpected and uncomfortable, yet it was undeniably crucial. It struck a nerve with Markus, the "Head" of the world's largest intelligence-gathering Agency.

The call served as a stark reminder of the immense responsibilities and high expectations that came with leading the Agency, an organization he so dearly loved. It also underscored a crucial reality: despite his significant role, he was ultimately just a cog in the vast machinery of the United States Government, subordinate to its most powerful leader—a man who took charge and needed no permission from anyone.

Max Sr. laughed as Markus hung up the phone, "So, let me see. Turn around for me." He motioned with his hand for Markus to spin around.

Markus looked confused and asked, "What?"

"I just wanted to see if the President handed your ass to you," Max Sr.'s laughter boomed even louder.

Markus shook his head in disgust as he redirected back to the Mission at hand.

Max Sr., Markus, and Elena sat around a hotel room table. They were looking over intel Mike had collected during his recon, as well as city maps and intel from Agent Caruso, including timetables for security sweeps, employee comings and goings, etc.

However, the most crucial intel had just been shared with Markus by the President of the United States moments ago. He was informed that a person of interest would be joining them shortly to provide additional details essential for the Mission. As it would turn out, this was someone they hadn't anticipated being involved. Not at all.

Mike entered the room, his expression etched with concern. His worry wasn't about the task ahead; on that front, he felt an excited sense of anticipation. Rather, his concern stemmed from the fear that Christina might have gleaned too much about his true profession. The thought of her worrying, coupled with his inability to provide comfort, weighed heavily on him. Causing her any distress was almost unbearable.

"Mike, what's wrong?" Elena immediately picked up on his troubled demeanor as soon as she laid eyes on him, a sight she found equally distressing to see on her spouse's face.

Mike simply shook his head, not wanting to delve into the details of his earlier conversation. Instead, he offered reassurance, "Nothing, Honey. It'll be alright."

Turning to Markus and his father, he quickly shifted focus to the Mission, "So, what do you think?"

Markus began to outline the strategy, "I think your plan will work. Max and I will enter from—"

Mike, surprised, cut him off mid-sentence, his tone firm, "Whoa, Markus. You and my dad aren't going to be anywhere near that building." He nodded towards Elena. "Elena and I can handle the General and his men. We need you two here to monitor the locals, nothing more."

Markus offered a restrained smile, countering Mike's directive, "Michael, perhaps you need a reminder that I don't take orders from you. It's actually the other way around. Your father and I will be there tonight."

Max Sr. stood up slowly, his expression echoing Markus's determination as he placed a reassuring hand on his shoulder. "It's alright, Markus. I've got this." He then turned to face his son with a stern look, "You, little shit!" This statement caught Mike off guard, causing him to reel back slightly. Max Sr. continued his voice firm, "I was kicking doors while you were still on the tit. You don't get to tell me what to do. Understood? I can still whoop your ass, boy. Don't force me to learn you. Copy?"

Mike's response, accompanied by a quiet chuckle, aimed to calm the situation. He slowly shook his head, acknowledging his father's irritation but sticking to his perspective. "Dad, I didn't mean it that way. I just meant that Elena and I got this. We're prepared for tonight. I really appreciate your willingness to help, but we need you here to keep an eye on it from this end. You know how things can go sideways."

Max Sr.'s response was straightforward, reflecting shock and determination at his son's reply. He nodded his head in agreement with Markus before addressing. "Son, don't take this the wrong way, but you're out of your damn mind if you think Markus and I aren't going to be involved tonight. And I'm not talking about just sitting here watching some computer screen. We'll be there, boots on the ground. I owe the General a face-to-face. And so does Markus, who, I remind you, is indeed your boss."

Mike couldn't help but be struck by more amusement and perhaps a bit of awe at his father's passionate insistence on being part of the action. Nevertheless, his resolve remained firm: he was not willing to put either his father or Markus—despite him being his boss—in any danger. As he was formulating a response to explain himself, a knock at the door provided a welcome reprieve, granting him a moment to gather his thoughts.

He walked over to the door and peered through the security peephole, his surprise evident. "What the hell is she doing here?" he muttered to himself as his hand caressed the door handle, preparing to face this unexpected visitor on the other side.

"Ciao, Michael. May I enter?" The Duchess, as always, was dressed impeccably, gracing the room with her confident stride. She walked past him, accompanied by Bigs and her head of security, Marco.

It hadn't been said who the President was sending to deliver the additional intel the team had requested, but now it was all too clear.

"Hello, Madam Prime Minister, it's so nice to see you again," Elena was the first to break the silence. The others were taken aback by her arrival. Unaware of Markus's recent conversation with the President, Mike was not yet privy to her involvement. Max Sr. and Markus just stood there, expressions blank, pondering the same question yet remaining silent until the Duchess smiled at them with her irresistibly charming grace.

"Ciao Bella, Elena, it is very nice to see you again, too," the Duchess responded warmly. She then turned to Max Sr., someone she hadn't seen in a very long time, "Master Chief Colburn, it is wonderful to see you again. It has been far too long."

Max Sr. responded warmly, "Yes, Fiamma, it has been far too long." He approached her, wrapping her in a warm embrace and tenderly kissing her cheek, an embrace and kiss that lasted ever so slightly too long.

The Duchess momentarily blushed, seemingly enjoying his touch, a reaction Mike immediately noticed, though not necessarily in a positive light. He thought, *There's no way my old man stepped out on my mom. Those two love each other more strongly than any couple I've ever seen. No, it couldn't be what you're thinking, Mike. No way.*

Curiosity getting the better of him, he asked, "So, how do you two know each other?" His tone was inquisitive, yet his gaze questioning.

Max Sr. and the Duchess shared a brief glance and a chuckle before he responded to his son's inquiry, "How about you just mind your business, boy, and leave it be."

This response only fueled Mike's suspicions, much to Max Sr.'s amusement. The Duchess then turned her attention to Markus, realizing she needed to clarify her presence. While revealing only the necessary details, she aimed to appease his growing curiosity.

"Markus, I understand my presence here may be surprising, but there is no need for concern. President Whitman and I are old friends. I come in peace, bringing information that I believe you will find interesting and, hopefully, useful."

Her words were set to serve dual purposes: imparting a history lesson and unfolding a narrative. She aimed to equip the team with the necessary knowledge to proceed with their Mission, all the while safeguarding certain "assets" that required a level of protection.

"Wei Yīngzhān, the older sister of Chinese President Mao Yīngzhān, played a pivotal role in his upbringing, acting as his surrogate mother during their formative years. Their father, Jian, a dedicated serviceman in the People's Liberation Army, was often called away for extended periods, leaving the siblings in the care of their grandmother in Qingyuan, a quaint village nestled in Wuyuan County, Jiangxi Province.

Tragedy struck early in their lives when a devastating fire claimed their mother, Wei, after whom the daughter was named. The blaze took not only the life of their beloved mother but also the village elders, leaving a void in the community's heart and leadership.

Faced with the loss, young Wei assumed the mantle of caregiver for her brother, a responsibility she embraced with the support of their grandparents. This early test of resilience and dedication forged a strong bond between the siblings and instilled in them a profound sense of duty and ambition.

Together, they matured into influential figures, each driven by a powerful determination to confront their nation's and the world's challenges. Wei quickly realized that the prevailing societal attitudes in China towards women would hinder her aspirations in the political arena. Nonetheless, her brother shared her enthusiasm and goals, and with Wei's guidance and support, he eagerly embarked on a political career.

Over the years, this powerful duo made significant strides within the Chinese political landscape. Mao's ascendancy was rapid, echoing the rise of his historical namesake, as he became one of the most formidable leaders in

China within an impressive span of 15 years. Yet, this ascent was not solely the result of Mao's efforts. Behind the scenes, it was his sister, the astute and fiercely loyal Wei, who masterfully maneuvered against any threats to their combined ambitions. Leveraging her intelligence and strategic acumen, she "neutralized" opponents and cleared the path for their "shared" vision, ensuring their goals were not only pursued but achieved.

Now, with President Mao firmly ensconced in his echelon of power, the true work of Wei Yīngzhān could commence.

A decade ago, Wei found her match on the other side of the world in the dynamic and energetic Lynda Thornfield Whitman. Lynda, at the time the spouse of the passionate Senator James T. Whitman, played a similar role to Wei. Acting as the pivotal force propelling James from a wounded Marine to one of the most influential Senators in the United States, with ambitions for even higher office.

Their paths crossed at a climate summit in Geneva, where Wei and Lynda, each formidable in her own right, recognized a kindred spirit in the other. Their interest wasn't rooted in friendship but in a mutual fascination with how the other navigated the complex world of politics and power. Both women sensed they might find themselves on opposing sides in the future, perhaps even as adversaries. However, at that moment, their priority was to probe and understand the depth of each other's strategic thinking and approach.

The duo engaged in a digital rendezvous weekly, indulging in the ultimate display of strategic prowess and foresight through the timeless game of chess. This ancient game, revered for centuries as the battleground of the world's most brilliant minds, became their chosen arena. In this virtual space, they tested each other's mettle, engaging in a cerebral dance of attack and defense, maneuvering and counter-maneuvering. Week after week, month after month, and year after year, their games unfolded with a precision that often led to a stalemate, a testament to their evenly matched intellects. Each move was calculated, each piece's fall meticulously planned, as they anticipated their opponent's strategies three or four movements in advance, turning their pawns into casualties of a grander scheme.

Despite the underlying tension in their relationship, the two women eventually formed a genuine bond. It was during a moment of vulnerability that Wei, grappling with heartache, confided in her once adversary. She revealed the turmoil in her personal life: her husband, the father of her three children, had been unfaithful. For Wei, a woman of impeccable intellect and resilience, the betrayal was a burden too heavy to bear. The deception became her albatross, weighing down her spirit and clouding her judgment.

In China, there's a saying, "Yuān yuān xiāng bào hé shí le," which loosely translates to, "When will the cycle of revenge end?" This phrase echoes a similar sentiment found in the familiar adage by William Congreve, "Hell hath no fury like a woman scorned." Both expressions underscore the depth of resolve and the lengths to which someone wronged will go to seek redress. Forged from this shared understanding, a pact was formed between the two women, uniting them in a common purpose: to right a grievous wrong, to mend what had been desperately fractured, and to enact the revenge that was so rightfully due. Together, these two formidable forces aligned against a mutual adversary, a man who would soon face the full measure of consequences for his actions.

The operational dynamics within the Chinese government are markedly different from those of the United States. In China, the President occupies a role similar to that of a dictator, with his decisions needing minimal, if any, external endorsements. However, there's a significant restraint on this autonomy: the Ministry of State Security (MSS). Serving as the Chinese Communist Party's (CCP) tool for oversight over the highest levels of authority, the MSS guarantees the party's survival under any circumstances. This structure posed a challenge to the plan devised by Wei and Lynda, as it limited the use of China's resources. Yet, the Chinese President had a unique advantage within the MSS. He alone possessed the authority to relocate agency employees at will, a capability that would prove extremely beneficial.

By this time, Lynda Whitman's position had evolved. No longer merely the wife of a U.S. Senator, she was now the ex-wife of the President of the United States, yet she retained influence over him. This connection opened up the resources of the most powerful nation on earth, placing at her disposal all the necessary tools not just to launch their meticulously planned operation but to ensure its resounding success.

Enter the one who could not only control the game of chess but effectively triumph before any pieces were even set on the board. Claire McHaskell was not just formidable; she was the mastermind whose strategies and foresight surpassed those of Wei, Lynda, and any other top strategist combined. Her involvement in the plan wasn't just an addition; it was the keystone that would turn an ambitious strategy into an inevitable triumph.

With her unparalleled intellect and ability to anticipate and manipulate outcomes, the trio became an unstoppable force, poised to execute a strategy that was as flawless in conception as it would be in "execution."

First, Huà Sūn, under the direct orders of President Mao, would be relocated to Italy—a country that, in recent years, had warmed to China, not adhering to the Western sentiment of keeping China at bay or criticizing the "ancestral land" for its stance on Taiwan. This move aligned with the One China Policy.

Second, a pawn would need to be sacrificed to facilitate the General's visit, giving him a reason to leave the security of China while also serving as cover for him and his lover to meet. Enter Alessandro Romano Vitali. His procurement of a particular item of Chinese interest provided the perfect bait.

For the trap to be effectively set in motion, the meticulous placement of each piece was paramount. Central to this elaborate arrangement was Claire. She alone would orchestrate the unfolding events from here on. Only her decisions would guide the plan to its intended fruition.

The third key element of the strategy involved The Director's un-knowing participation.

A month before Mike and Christina's anniversary was Markus's birthday. Claire extended an invitation for him to join them in Texas to celebrate with his adopted family and godchildren. Markus, a man defined by his disciplined lifestyle, abstained from common indulgences such as drinking, smoking, or any form of drug use. He maintained his fitness with precision and adhered strictly to health advice from his doctors. Yet, amidst this regimented existence, Markus harbored a singular passion that brought vibrancy to his life: his love for motorcycles. Fast motorcycles.

His collection was nothing short of extraordinary, featuring a diverse array of the world's most exhilarating machines. Italian superbikes like Ducati, British classics from Triumph and Langen, American icons including Harley Davidson and Indian Motorcycles, as well as the pinnacle of speed from Japanese giants such as Suzuki, Yamaha, and Honda, all found a place in his meticulously maintained garage. This collection was more than a hobby; it was a testament to Markus's pursuit of excitement and precision engineering, a rare glimpse into the personal joys of a man so often cloaked in the seriousness of his profession.

Although Claire found motorcycles unsafe and had forbidden Mike from owning one, she was always intrigued watching Markus's enthusiasm when he spoke of the sport. His excitement about contemplating his next purchase and researching every facet was palpable. This gave Claire an idea for the next stage of her plan.

For his latest acquisition, a fire-engine red Ducati Panigale V4, Claire bought him a matching leather jacket as a birthday gift.

Unbeknownst to many, manufacturers of motorcycle jackets have traditionally included a specific item, usually sewn into the fabric over the left-hand side of the chest. This object, considered by some more a token of superstition than anything else, was meant to watch over the rider and ensure safe travels in their endeavors.

Claire, or rather Christina's choice, was exactly what Markus had hoped for in his gift. Upon opening the box, he couldn't resist trying it on to see how it fit. Slipping his left arm through, he felt the unmistakable shape of the article. But unlike tradition, it wasn't sewn into the jacket; instead, it was placed inside a specially designed open pocket on the inside. Curious about the item, Markus quickly retrieved it, and upon laying eyes on it, he felt as if his world had been turned upside down.

In his grasp, he held a metallic medallion depicting a heroic man, his muscular frame and long, flowing beard, carrying a child upon his shoulder while holding a sturdy staff in his hand.

The fourth key element involved a more nuanced figure: Max Sr., Mike's adopted father and Claire's father-in-law.

Having retired years prior, Max Sr. found the management of Mike's finances, alongside Dave Black, to be more demanding than he had anticipated. With Bailey now assuming that responsibility, Max Sr. was free to pursue his passions, one of which was golf. His affinity for the sport began in Kuwait during Operation Desert Storm, where the lush greens provided a stark contrast to the arid desert surrounds. This experience ignited a lasting love for the game, leading him to enjoy peaceful rounds more frequently.

A week ago, Max Sr. found himself in the company of three old Navy buddies, playing the back nine at Torrey Pines, his preferred course in his hometown of San Diego, California. Surprisingly, his friends had all won a free tee time at the renowned course, complete with $500 in spending money and all travel expenses covered for those living out of state. None of the men could recall entering any contest, but they were all delighted by their unexpected victory.

As often happens when old friends gather, their conversations meandered through memories, eventually dwelling on comrades they had lost. It wasn't long before their collective thoughts converged on a singular figure—a man whose bravery had once saved them all. At the clubhouse, following their game, five drinks were purchased, but only four were consumed. With their glasses raised high, a heartfelt toast resonated through the room as each man paid homage to their fallen brothers, expressing gratitude for the sacrifices that allowed them to return to their families. "To Juan, Petey, and Chris. Godspeed, brothers!" they declared, their voices laden with reverence and a touch of sorrow.

Less than five days later, Markus and Max Sr. soared through the skies aboard the Director's private jet, bound for their rendezvous with destiny.

After learning about the circumstances surrounding the death of Christina's father and identifying who was ultimately responsible for the act, Claire realized that it was Mike who needed to avenge Senior Chief Petty Officer Christopher Canepa's death.

Consequently, it was about a week later, after Claire had learned of the General's involvement, that Wei Yīngzhān had come to understand her husband's extracurricular activities.

The General was a very careful man; his affair with Ms. Sūn had spanned many years. It wasn't until a simple mistake was made that his fate was sealed. In China, they have a day similar to St. Valentine's Day in the States, the Qixi Festival, celebrated on the 7th day of the 7th month of the Chinese lunar calendar. On this day, just like in the U.S., it's customary for men to buy sweets for their love. General Fung Wu, adhering to tradition, did just that. He ordered chocolates from Paris, one box for his wife of many years and another sent to the love of his life, Huà Sūn. However, this is where things went south for the good General. Huà Sūn was diabetic, which meant she could not ingest sugar; however, his wife was not. A simple "shipping error" sent the wrong box to the wrong woman. It didn't take long for Wei to piece together what was really going on. Days later, with the help of her American friend, the plan was in motion.

The table was set, and the chessboard was ready for the final contest. Everything had been arranged; now, it was time for the Mission to come to fruition. **Checkmate.**

Of course, the Duchess did not actually divulge the true masterminds of the story; instead, only two individuals would receive credit, and neither were female.

"So you see, President Whitman and President Yīngzhān have taken care of everything. No military or embassy personnel will be present tonight when you arrive. However, the General's personal guards will be in place. We currently count six men, all stationed on the floors below and above the General's quarters. He made it a point to clear the rear staircase for his girlfriend to enter undetected. I believe that is your best entrance point. For the others, you will have to make on-the-spot decisions as you go. The General has also disabled all security cameras. This move is likely intended to prevent any unwanted scrutiny, ensuring his true intentions remain hidden from prying eyes."

Mike, Max Sr., and Elena were truly surprised by the complexity and ingenuity of the Mission's planning. Mike, in particular, felt a surge of admiration for the President. The intricacy of the operation and the collaboration with a counterpart he hadn't even known the President was in communication with left him astounded.

Markus, however, was far less impressed by the President's purported involvement. He quickly deduced that James Whitman and Mao Yīngzhān had minimal to no actual participation in the orchestration of this scheme. His blunt burst of, "My God,... that woman is diabolical," drew curious looks from the others.

"What, Markus?" Max Sr. inquired, seeking clarification.

The Director quickly deflected, "Sorry, I was lost in thought." He then addressed the Duchess, "Fiamma, thank you for everything. I believe we're equipped to take it from here. I think it would be best if this operation had as little of your direct involvement as possible from now on."

"Of course, Markus, you are right," agreed the Duchess, acknowledging his point. She turned to Mike, "My man will stay with you until the task is complete. Use him as you see fit." Her gaze shifted to Biagio, "Mr. Caruso, I expect that we did not see each other here tonight. Are we clear?"

"Sì, Signora, we understand each other," Bigs replied, confirming their mutual agreement.

Mike turned to the Duchess, their eyes locking. She understood his thoughts before he could voice them and sought to address his concerns preemptively. "Amore mio, it is I who should apologize. You and I had no future, a truth you would have seen had your vision not been so obscured by the moment," her tone was laced with gentle regret. She offered a warm smile to Elena, then turned her gaze back to Mike, "You have been blessed with a family worthy of the gods. I wish you nothing but joy and happiness. My love."

With that, the Duchess made her exit as gracefully as she had entered, signaling that the Mission was a go.

Ashes to Ashes:

The Team arrived at the Casa d'Acquavite Lombardi building just before 11:00 pm, moments before Huà Sūn was scheduled to arrive. Of course, due to the "circumstances," her arrival would have been impossible.

As previously mentioned, the Lombardi building had been a longstanding distillery, providing the people of Milan and the wider world with fine brandy for over a century. Throughout its history, the building had its fair share of close calls. During World War II, it was shelled—albeit accidentally—by Allied warplanes attempting to dislodge German occupiers from the city and surrounding areas. This led to a fire that consumed the top floors. Witnesses described flames rising into the sky, visible from afar, as burning barrels of the fine liquor glowed bright blue, casting an eerie light over the city for hours before the inferno was finally brought under control.

Despite the potential for extensive damage, the building stood firm. A decade later, an accidental spill once again set the storied distillery ablaze. This time, with government services quickly mobilized, only minor damage occurred.

These were not the facility's only brushes with fire; locals recount at least eight instances where the historic structure was engulfed in flames.

Finally, in the early 2000s, the Lombardi family decided they had endured enough. With heavy hearts and somber expressions, they closed the distillery's doors for the final time.

Years went by, and the building remained empty, declared unsuitable for habitation. The local government eventually decided to schedule it for demolition to make way for much-needed housing. However, this plan was halted by an unexpected offer from the Chinese Government to purchase the building, which proposed an amount considered excessively high for such a dilapidated structure. Over the years, countless spills of alcohol had seeped into the building's wooden framework, from floors to pillars, rendering almost every inch saturated with the volatile liquid. This propensity for flammability was why it had caught fire so many times in the past and why it was now deemed uninhabitable.

Although the spirits had long since evaporated, reducing the immediate dangers, years of permeation had forever altered the wood at a molecular level. The structure's antique timber elements, having been soaked in the solvent, developed tiny pores that became ideal environments for certain fungi. These living organisms, which couldn't survive while the liquor's vapors lingered, now thrived in the absence of the intoxicating beverage.

Enter Pyrospora fermentum. A seemingly benign species of fungus that originated from the aging cellars at Casa d'Acquavite had spread throughout the entire building. Under normal circumstances, such an organism wouldn't have posed significant health risks. Yet, this particular strain adapted uniquely to the microclimate shaped by centuries of brandy production.

Distinct from the common wood decay fungi that lead to rot, Lombardi's Pyrospora fermentum possessed a remarkable metabolic pathway. It metabolized the alcohol residues embedded within the wood's pores, leading to the accelerated and highly efficient production of methane.

This gas, far more flammable than the alcohol vapors that once saturated the structure, presented significant risks. Its explosive nature was a cause for concern, but even more alarming were the potentially deadly effects on humans unknowingly exposed to concentrated methane levels.

This led the Italian government to deem the building uninhabitable. However, Chinese engineers devised a simple but ingenious plan: ventilate the gas.

By installing large air-moving fans on each floor, along with sizable methane scrubbers, they made the building safe for human occupancy once again. The risk of fire was significantly reduced, and the health concerns associated with methane's toxic effects on the human body were nullified. A straightforward solution requiring minimal investment, it was a win-win situation. This setup also presented Mike with the opportunity he had been seeking.

Tonight, the storied building was to witness another act of violence. This time, the threat wouldn't come from the sky above but would infiltrate from its very core.

Positioned at the back of the building, Mike meticulously reviewed the plan. According to their updated intelligence, consulate personnel and military guards were supposed to be absent from their posts, and this was verified upon their arrival. Also confirmed was the sighting of a few MSS bodyguards, visible through the windows above, in the spaces that the former distillery had been transformed—now serving as a combination of office space and living quarters.

"Alright, so the General's men are there as expected. No problem." Mike turned to Elena, "When we enter, I'll take the men on the left. You cover from below and provide..."

Max Sr., again not wanting to be sidelined, cut in, "Son, the orders have been given. Markus and I will breach. And make no mistake, I'm not here to observe." Gesturing towards Markus, he added, "We will handle the guards. You go straight for the General. Once things kick off, he'll likely try to bolt, and you know that all too well."

Mike and General Wu's first encounter was a tale often retold, though not by Mike, who didn't quite relish the memory. General Wu, on the other hand, enjoyed adding his own flair to the story.

SSO Markus Delphy, this time working with Mike and his team, had uncovered intelligence indicating that the Chinese were once again supplying the Taliban with strategic information. Frustrated by these actions, the Brass decided it was time to intervene. Mike and SEAL Team ECHO were dispatched to neutralize the threat. This, unbeknownst to Mike at the time, marked his last operation as Team leader and concluded his tenure in the Navy.

General Wu had positioned himself and his operatives in the Spin Ghar Mountains along the border with Pakistan. From this vantage point, they could oversee the activities below, where Taliban leaders frequently visited to receive updates on enemy troop movements.

On that fateful day, a convoy from Her Majesty's Royal Army was en route to a remote outpost for resupply, unaware that Chinese intelligence had pinpointed their movements. This led to a fierce engagement with Taliban forces, leaving the British soldiers vastly outnumbered and outgunned.

However, one significant result emerged from this cowardly attack: the precise location of General Wu was discovered. Utilizing U.S. surveillance and time-lapse imagery, a sort of playback led American forces directly to the General's hideout.

Mike and his team were relentless. "If it moves, we kill it," were the stark orders they operated under.

General Wu had underestimated the vulnerability of his security within the caves. After years of extended conflict with the Taliban, U.S. forces had become adept at deciphering their strategies and the tactics used in constructing the cave systems. "It was like shooting fish in a barrel," one of the valiant sailors on the team would later describe during hearings on the operation.

Mike, along with his brothers Max Jr. and Ricky, had thoroughly combed through the last section of the area, but General Wu remained elusive. Despite the intelligence reports pinpointing his location within the cave system, he was nowhere to be found. Mike, determined and unyielding in what he deemed a critical part of the Mission, pushed deeper into the labyrinth of caves, his brothers in tow, each fueled by a fierce desire to "capture" the elusive Chinese General.

It was at this juncture that Mike's career would take a dramatic turn.

General Dale McMasters, the Marine commander overseeing the sector and the operation's commanding officer, issued a stand-down order. He declared the Mission's objectives met, arguing there was no further need to risk the lives of "his men." He ordered, "ECHO 1 Return to Base (RTB) immediately for debrief."

This directive did not sit well with Mike and his team. True to his nature and reflective of his actions, both past and present, Mike chose to defy the direct order. Ignoring General McMasters' explicit instructions, he pressed forward, embodying the very defiance and resolve that had defined his military career and, some would say, his way of life.

Moments later, the team had cornered General Wu, who was frantically attempting to evade capture. Described mockingly as hiding "like a little *bitch*" in the darkness. The General was suddenly illuminated by the team's infrared vision. Mike, with a cold smile, had his rifle trained on the target that he believed deserved his retribution.

The Taliban's proficiency in crafting and deploying Improvised Explosive Devices (IEDs) was a well-known hazard. The Team's specialists were tasked with neutralizing such threats to ensure safe passage, but Mike, driven by a thirst for vengeance, had not waited for the all-clear. His impetuous advance was characteristic. His judgment clouded by his insatiable bloodlust.

General Wu, fully aware that his pursuer's focus was singularly on him, capitalized on his potential oversight. A strategically thrown rock became his savior. The resulting explosion was devastating in the confined space, sending shrapnel screaming through the air in all the right directions.

A fragment struck Mike with precision, embedding itself in his L3 vertebrae. The force of the blast knocked him off his feet, rendering the would-be executioner incapacitated. The Mission was momentarily derailed, and Mike's pursuit of vengeance was abruptly halted by the very tactics they had sought to overcome.

The unforeseen aftermath of the blast was not entirely in General Wu's favor. While he managed to disrupt his imminent demise and hopefully "permanently" incapacitate one of his would-be assassins, the chaos of war spared no one. The shrapnel, those hot, jagged projectiles of metal, found another mark in the darkness.

A piece tore across General Wu's face, slicing through his right cheek before it mercilessly invaded his right eye, ultimately lodging itself in his skull. This grim souvenir of battle would leave him permanently maimed, robbing him of the use of his right eye. The IED, indiscriminate in its destruction, thus claimed another, altering the General's life irrevocably. His vision forever diminished, a constant reminder of the narrow escape from death and embedding the image of Senior Chief Michael McHaskell in his psyche.

General Wu managed to escape as Mike's SEAL team brothers scrambled to evacuate their leader to safety. A month later, Mike and General Mc-Masters faced off for their final confrontation. Mike had disobeyed a direct order, and there would be consequences for such an act of insubordination. Now back on his feet, Mike took steps that would ultimately seal his fate, striking General McMasters with all the force he could muster.

General Wu took certain liberties in recounting his version of "Besting the best the Americans had to offer," spinning tales of heroism and his unwavering commitment to his people and his sacrifice. In a way, it was true. His actions did indeed remove one of the United States' greatest warriors from the playing field, but events hadn't unfolded as his newfound fiction suggested.

For Mike, he found himself in the embrace of The Company, which led him to this moment – ready to rectify a wrong from his past. The Mission was clear: the total and unequivocal eradication of General Fung Wu.

"Yes, Dad, you're right. You and Markus follow me in. Elena, you cover our six." Mike then turned to Bigs and Marco, both men poised and ready for action. "When we move, you're on lookout. Neutralize anyone who might interfere. So far, the General's men are positioned on the top and second floors, but stay frosty; we can't be sure of that." Back to the team, he continued, "We have fifteen minutes to get in and get out once Bigs cuts the ventilation. Time will be against us. Everyone solid?"

Elena looked puzzled, prompting him to ask, "You got this?"

She shook her head. It wasn't that she was confused about the plan — on that, she was gold. It was something Mike had mentioned on their way to the Mission site that had her wondering. She asked, "Mike, you said not to worry about Christina. That you had it covered, that you took care of her, and she wouldn't be leaving the hotel room. What did you mean by that?"

He glanced at his watch, clearly irritated by the distraction. Huà Sūn was due to arrive in five minutes, and with each passing second, there was a risk the General might get spooked. He simply brushed off her concern, which, of course, didn't sit well with his wife. Elena asked again, this time with a bit more, let's just say, zest, "Michael, what did you mean by 'I took care of her?'"

Shaking his head, Mike realized he needed to explain. The team was ready; Bigs had just cut the power to the building's ventilation system, and they were now on the clock. "Elena, this isn't the time or place, but I just meant that I slipped her something to help her sleep, that's all. Don't worry, she will be fine. I got it from Doc Hansen; it's nothing like what he gave you in Switzerland. Believe me, I would never make that mistake again." He turned toward the door, readying the team for entry.

However, Elena had other plans. She pulled him by the shoulder to face her and addressed him in a whispered but forceful tone, "You did what?!" Before he could react, she coiled her right arm back and unloaded on her husband with everything she had. The force of her fist, tight with anger, struck Mike on the left side of his jaw, stunning the giant man into silence. But that didn't last long.

"Elena, what the hell," Mike, unable to keep his voice to a whisper, recoiled, holding his now bleeding mouth. "Why?..."

Elena was already on her phone, frantically dialing. She held her hand up as if to quiet the whining "baby" from speaking.

A voice answered the call, "Hello, Doctor Hansen, it's Elena Jones... I understand, but I need to speak with you. You gave Mike a prescription for some sleeping pills... Yes, those ones. I need to know if there will be any risk to the person he gave them to. Here's the rundown: twenty-one years old, approximately ninety-five pounds, pregnant roughly six weeks..." She spoke quickly and waited for an answer with a few "Okay's and yes'," interspersed.

Now, it was Mike's turn to look confused. He tried to interject into the conversation, "Elena, Christina, and I just started trying again to get pregnant..."

Elena, with a finger pointed up at him, pressed her hand on his mouth with a harsh, "Shhh, I'm on the phone."

She continued, still at a whisper. "Great, Doctor, thank you. And any long-term issues, you know, with the baby?"

Doctor Hansen assured her that Christina should be fine, but he wanted her to give her vitamin B6 and B12 injections. "Not that I am too worried, Agent Jones, but I would feel better if you could."

"Of course, Doctor, I'll do that right away. Thank you. I'll call if I have any other questions."

Doctor Hansen replied, "I'll be by the phone. Please let me know if there's anything you need." He paused for a second, "My God, Mike did it agai n..."

"Yes, he did. Okay, Doctor, I'll get it done." Elena's eyes reddened with fury before she spoke. Trying to control herself, she quickly lost that battle. She reared back again. This time, Mike winced, which calmed the fuming Latina. "You idiot!" she yelled, still muffled but not by much, "What gave you the right to do something like this to our Christina? Who do you think you are? Mike, if I didn't love you..." She closed her eyes and tried to calm down before continuing, "Look, you didn't know; I get that, but never again! I mean it! If I ever find out that you do something like this to one of us again..."

Max Sr., assuming command of the situation, directed, "Elena, we've got this. Go and look after my new grandbaby."

Elena gave her father-in-law a nod in acknowledgment, "Yes, Sir, stay safe. Mike, you really are an idiot..." Letting out a sigh, she continued, "But don't worry, I'll fix this," her voice tinged with a mix of disappointment and frustration. She couldn't help but let out a soft growl as she turned to leave.

Mike and Markus stood there, stunned, watching her storm off, hands waving in the air. She didn't make any sound, but they knew what she was thinking—anyone who saw her would.

Markus glanced at Mike with a questioning tone and asked, "Congratulations?"

Again, Mike didn't respond; he was lost in thought, doubting his own judgment once more.

For Bigs and Marco, accustomed to such "strong-willed" women, this was nothing new. They both smiled at each other and readied for the task at hand.

"Son, she'll be fine. Keep your head in the game," Max Sr. reassured, noticing Mike's now changed demeanor.

"Roger that, Dad," he replied, back on Mission, albeit not as focused as before. He had a "date" with the General, and he was keeping it.

The rear door was open as foretold. The General had turned off the cameras so his lover could enter undetected. True to the Duchess's word, no guards were on the lower floors. The building seemed empty. Mike was the first to enter the stairwell, followed by Max Sr., then Markus covering the rear. The men were dressed in tactical blacks and plate holders. Bigs had provided them with Chinese weaponry. Mike wished he had his trusty tools. Every warrior knows you never go into battle with untested equipment, but this was a necessary evil.

It didn't take long for the first trial of his sidearm. A single shot rang out. Although it was silenced, it was still loud enough to alert the General.

"God damn Chinese piece of shit," Mike muttered, breaking formation and prompting Max Sr. and Markus to follow. He quickly directed the men to the hallways on the third floor using only hand signals, bypassing the second floor and leaving those areas for Bigs and Marco to handle. He was determined to reach the General's quarters quickly, not giving the man any time to run "like a little bitch" again.

Without his backup, he approached the General's door. Not knowing what awaited him and throwing all caution to the wind, he smashed it with all the force his 6'5", 300-pound frame could summon. The door shattered into pieces. Mike, now with his rifle at the ready, charged in, prepared to take on anyone in his path.

To his surprise, and, frankly, the General's astonishment, there were only two men in the room—and one was Mike.

General Wu, caught in his birthday suit, lay on the bed in a pose that could only be described as "compromised," as if he had been expecting a very different kind of visitor. Realizing the error, the General lunged for his nightstand.

But Mike was there in a flash, slamming the man's hand into the open drawer. The General yelled out in pain. Then, Mike took aim at his left leg. Turning the rifle butt first, he delivered a forceful jab. The impact struck the General's shin, producing a sound akin to exploding wood. However, it wasn't wood. Seconds later, another sound filled the room. This time, it was the General, whose right hand wasn't his only wound. He now had a visibly shattered leg to contend with.

Max Sr. and Markus quickly "subdued" the only two guards on the floor. Each landed swift, precise shots, taking the men down in a double-tap succession, with Max Sr. concluding the skirmish with a shot to the forehead of both men. Hearing the commotion from the open bedroom doorway, they headed in to back up Mike.

Entering the General's quarters was a sight Max Sr. would never forget; there, he saw the man that Markus, Max Jr., and Ricky knew – not the son he had raised.

Mike's eyes were as black as tar, and a smile spread across his face. His teeth, still smeared with blood from Elena's earlier punishment, added a sinister tone to his demeanor. Yes, the General was going to die that night; of this, all were certain. But the question remained: how would he meet his end?

"Once again, Agent McHaskell, it seems you have me at a disadvantage," the General remarked, a somewhat disturbing smile on his face. Despite facing his inevitable demise, he seemed unfazed, as if it didn't bother him at all.

This didn't deter Mike from his Mission. He answered, "Yes, it seems so, General." Motioning to the General's bleeding leg with a grin, he continued, "At least I know you won't be running away this time."

General Wu replied with a resigned look, "Yes, I do believe you are quite right. If only I had a rock."

Turning to Max Sr. and Markus, he continued, "Master Chief Colburn, it has been a long time. I presume your presence signifies a quest for vengeance for your comrades. Tragic, the manner of their demise, was it not? Such vitality extinguished in their prime. As the adage holds, war is the very embodiment of hell. Would you not agree, Mr. Director?"

Max Sr. had to muster all his self-control to resist the urge to pull the trigger right then and there. And yet, it wasn't time. The man had to suffer for his crimes, and that was the main reason the Master Chief was there – to make sure he suffered... and greatly. "Yes, General, it has been a long time. I believe the last time we met, you were only a colonel, isn't that right?"

"Ahh, yes, you are correct, Master Chief. In fact, I owe you a debt of gratitude. By delivering the demise of YOUR elite American warriors to my countrymen, they found it impossible not to award me with my first star. So for that, I do indeed, thank you." The General spat out a malevolent laugh.

Markus had remained silent since the conversation started. He didn't know what to say. He knew the men's, his friends' deaths were his fault. That if he had done his job faster, better, they would all be alive today. This guilt was his burden and his alone.

"And you, Mr. Director, I must confess, your presence here puzzles me..." The General paused momentarily before continuing, "Ahh, of course, now it comes back to me. Well, sometimes we simply find ourselves on the losing side, Markus. That day, you were the one who faced defeat, and I emerged victorious. You know, upon further reflection, it appears that your actions also led to your comrades' suffering losses." With a self-satisfied grin, he added, "And what of the young woman? Let me remember... Yes, the wife of the Senior Chief Canepa, who had just welcomed their child into the world. Did you look after her, Markus, as you vowed you would?" Seeing the surprised expression on Markus's face, he couldn't resist adding, "Truly, Mr. Director, did you really believe I was oblivious to your pledge? Your house is not in order, my old friend."

Mike had heard enough; for the General to even have his Christina's mention in his mouth was too much. With another forceful blow, the General's second leg met the same fate as his first. A scream echoed, marking a shift in the General's demeanor. The end was near.

"Actually, General, she has a wonderful life. She's a wife and mother. Things for her turned out perfectly. However, for you? I think not so much." Markus smiled back at the man who had shaped his life. Maybe not for the better, but he had, nonetheless. "I have a message from Wei. I think you should hear it before..." His smile grew even wider before continuing, "Well,... you know."

"My beloved Wei?" Finally, the look on the General's face changed, his mind racing.

"Yes, she wanted you to hear these words before I let Mike here finish the job. 'Nǐ de bèipàn, huì zài nǐ de sǐwáng zhōng zhǎodào zhōngjié.' (Your betrayal will find its end in your death.)"

The General's face said it all; this was a planned execution, down to the last words he would hear. Gone were the smug glances and the seemingly triumphant boasts. Now, nothing but fear resided in his heart.

Max Sr. removed a metal item from his pocket and handed it to Markus. The men looked at each other with a smile. Markus had a small tear in his right eye as he gazed down at the chrome-plated Zippo. With a small chuckle, he read the engraving, "To Petey, may this spark more warmth than your 'small Petey' ever could – your brothers."

With one fluid motion, he flicked open the lighter's top, igniting the wick. His expression was a complex tapestry of satisfaction and finality, a grim smile playing upon his lips. Then, with a calculated toss, he flung the lighter onto the bed. Instantaneously, flames leaped to life, eagerly consuming the mattress. The fibers, soaked in low levels of methane gas, became a voracious inferno. Within moments, the room was filled with the harrowing sound of terror-filled screams. The General, caught in the heart of the blaze, was now ensnared in the throes of his grisly end.

The three men recoiled from the advancing flames, their gazes fixed as the General's body contorted in agony, his screams piercing the air. Mike glanced toward his father and Markus, noting the stark satisfaction carved into their faces as the General was consumed by fire. Despite his initial desire for personal vengeance, he understood the significance of their collective presence at the General's demise. At that moment, witnessing the end of their adversary was all that mattered.

As the General's suffering intensified, Markus's inherent compassion surfaced. Instinctively, he aimed his rifle to swiftly end the torment. But Max Sr. intervened with a gentle firmness. Placing his hand on the barrel, he guided it downward while shaking his head in a silent "no." The message was clear: the General's fate was to be consumed by the flames, a grim recompense for his sins, his final atonement.

Once celebrated for its old-world craftsmanship, the Casa d'Acquavite Lombardi building would not escape its fate. Tonight, the sky above would be lit for the final time.

Happy Anniversary, Mike:

Christina's smile brightened the room as she opened her eyes, greeted by the sight of her husband sitting on the bed, smiling down at her. Overwhelmed with affection, he couldn't resist wrapping her in a warm embrace and showering her with kisses. His love for her was so profound it bordered on pain.

"Happy anniversary, husband," she greeted, returning his affection with a kiss.

"Happy anniversary, my wife," Mike echoed. He then retrieved the item she had entrusted to him the night before. He carefully fastened it around her neck. "Babe, thank you for this. It kept me safe last night."

Christina's eyes welled with tears—not from sorrow, but from the overwhelming love she felt for Mike and the fear that one day he might not return. "My dad was a good man, wasn't he, Mike?"

"He was, Sweetheart, he really was." Mike's voice was a soft affirmation, a soothing balm to her worries.

"Hey, Elena came in here last night and gave me a shot in my bottom. Actually, I think she gave me two. I was sound asleep. They hurt!"

Mike, looking to find the source of her discomfort, gently rolled her over and responded, "Oh yeah? Where, Honey? I'll kiss it and make it better."

Christina, with a pouty expression, pointed to her backside, "Right here."

"Hmm, let me see," he leaned over and planted a kiss, "Did that make it all better?"

"Well, yeah, but it also hurts here," she indicated to the other side.

Continuing his tender care, he kissed her again, this time on the opposite side of her bottom.

Christina then rolled onto her back, playfully pointing to other areas where she desired his "kisses."

Mike smiled, indulging her requests, "Of course, my Queen. Your wish is my command."

Later that morning, Mike made his way to the bedroom where Elena had been staying. To his dismay, her clothes were gone, and all her possessions had disappeared as if she had never been there. No note was left behind, but the message was clear. With a heavy heart, he returned to the room that housed the love of his life.

"So, what do you want to do today?" he asked. Christina was in the midst of getting dressed, and she had already laid out his outfit on the bed.

"We need to go for a photo shoot today, my King," she laughed, fully aware that this wasn't an activity Mike would particularly enjoy. However, he was unaware of all the surprises she had planned for him.

Of course, Mike felt deflated but would have done anything for her. "Sounds... 'Fun,'" he replied, his enthusiasm wrapped in layers of sarcasm.

With Bailey's help, Christina had arranged a spectacular gift for her husband. That day, they met with the legendary Marco Lucatelli, the founder of Velocità Re Motors, renowned for producing the fastest-production supercars in the world. The power couple had made a notable impression in the fashion world and were now in high demand. Mike, of course, didn't want to comply and asked Christina to find a way to release him from this commitment, which she managed to do. Nevertheless, the gift remained. For her involvement, the couple was rewarded with a Velocità Re Fulmine GT.

The Velocità Re Fulmine GT, the pinnacle of Italian engineering and design, boasted a 6.5L V12 engine that produced an astounding 800 horsepower. It achieved a top speed of 220 mph (354 km/h) and could accelerate from 0 to 60 in just 2.8 seconds. Its design was a perfect blend of sleek, aerodynamic lines and aggressive styling, featuring a distinctive front grille that set it apart from any other car on the road. This marvel of automotive technology and artistry was not just a car; it was a statement of luxury, speed, and the culmination of Italian craftsmanship. Now, it was all Mike's.

"Oh my God, Babe! I can't believe this. Thank you so much!" Mike was beside himself when Lucatelli presented the work of art to him.

"Your Christina, she is simply magnificent, Mr. McHaskell. I only wish I had a woman with half her charm. Please, enjoy your new masterpiece. As I know you will."

Still stunned by the amazing gift, Mike could only reply, "Thank you, Mr. Lucatelli, I definitely will."

Christina, on a first-name basis with Marco Lucatelli, threw him a wink, thanking him. And while Mike couldn't hear her, she made arrangements for the future. Just like her relationship with "The Maestro" Lorenzo

Cavallaro, the two had struck a deal. But for now, Mike wasn't in the "need to know" category. *Just let him have his day*, she thought.

This wasn't the only surprise Christina had in store for her husband. Tonight, she had planned an intimate dinner, served in the hotel suite, just the two of them, alone. Or so she told him.

"Babe, you look amazing! Really, wow, Honey, just wow." Mike was changing into his tux, another of Christina's additions to his wardrobe. She had already gotten ready and needed to put the finishing touches on the evening's events.

"Thank you, Honey. When you're done, meet me in the living room," she said, helping him with his jacket. Mike winced when he moved his right arm; his ribs were still sore. Christina had noticed it, of course, but didn't show it, that was until now. He had stuck to his "wearing of a t-shirt" strategy, not fooling her for a second. "When we get home, you're having those ribs looked at. This is not up for debate. I'll see you in a minute," she added, walking out of the bedroom.

When Mike opened the door to the living area of the suite, he was amazed. He had heard noises coming from outside the bedroom but had no idea what she had planned.

"Happy Anniversary, my husband!" Christina's larger-than-life smile was on full display as she motioned to a table set for two. Adorned with the finest silverware money could buy, it gleamed in the light, with all the food he loved staring back at him. But what was even more exciting were the two large TVs set up at one end of the table, with a webcam in the center.

"What is all this, Babe?" he asked.

Christina motioned to his chair, pulling it out for him, and responded, "Just sit here, and I'll show you."

After he was seated, Christina nodded to a waiter standing in the hallway. He, in turn, nodded to another person sitting behind a computer. The monitors came to life, and the images on the screen instantly brought Mike to tears.

"My family! My beautiful family. Hello, everyone! Hello!" he cried out.

Before them was a live feed from Texas, showing Claire, Parker, and Bailey all dressed for a night of memories. They were surrounded by the McHaskell children, who were dressed just like their mothers – elegant, the little boys in their tuxedos, matching their father.

"Hello! There's Daddy!" followed by choruses of "Daddy" and the mumblings of toddlers, as well as the cries of newborns. Sounds that swelled his heart.

"Babe, this is amazing... Thank you so much. Hello, everyone!" he cried again.

Christina, now as choked up as her husband, added, "Honey, this isn't all I have for you tonight." She turned to the monitors and her family. "Everyone, I have some wonderful news," turning back to Mike, she continued, "Husband, you are going to be a daddy once more. I'm pregnant!."

Loud cheers from Texas filled the room as Mike broke down into tears. His life had come together in the best way possible. Yes, life was great for Mike McHaskell, all due to the women who made it so special. He embraced Christina with all he had, kissing her passionately.

"Happy anniversary, Mike."

"Happy anniversary, Christina."

Thank you for joining us on the latest adventure, "Ashes to Ashes," in the Mike McHaskell Series. We hope you found this new, more streamlined version captivating. For the latest updates, visit our website at marshallblack.com and consider subscribing to our newsletter for early peeks at what's coming soon.

Next in line, "The Healer" presents Mike McHaskell in a challenging new light. Aligned with an old friend in the Texas Rangers, Mike is on a Mission to right a wrong. Faced with a clash between his evolving morals and the instincts of his former self, which path will he choose? Discover Mike's next steps in "The Healer," debuting in Summer 2024.

Your enjoyment of our novels fuels our passion. The greatest compliment you can give us is sharing our stories with others. If our books have captured your imagination, we'd be honored if you'd help spread the word.

From my family to yours, a heartfelt thank you for your continued support.

-Marshall

V1030524

Made in the USA
Columbia, SC
15 September 2024

5be7b678-7040-4995-8e7b-4159a0c0014bR02